THE COLD CALL KILLER

A chilling crime thriller with a stunning final twist

EMMY ELLIS

DI Bethany Smith Book 1

Originally published as *Cold is the Caller*

JOFFE BOOKS

Revised edition 2023
Joffe Books, London
www.joffebooks.com

First published in Great Britain in 2019
as *Cold is the Caller*

This paperback edition was first published
in Great Britain in 2023

Cover art by Dee Dee Book Covers

ISBN: 978-1-83526-103-3

PROLOGUE

Wounds. They remain as scars.
Always there. Reminders.

"What's your emergency?"

"I killed a man."

"Where?"

"In his house."

"Sir, where is that?"

"In his street."

"What's your name, sir?"

"Fuck off."

T slammed the phone down, laughing his damn head off. What a bloody rush.

Leaning over the waist-height wall beside the river, he let go of the mobile, the plop of it hitting the murky water satisfying, just like it had been when he'd dropped the other thing in five minutes ago. Then he got in his van and sped off along the city streets, giggling, a thread of euphoria streaking through his body. Life was good, wasn't it, when you decided to bump off all the people who'd pissed you off, hurt you, hurt your sister?

Yeah, it was good all right.

Georgia would be home off the night shift in a few hours. She'd find that dead bastard and crap her knickers. What he'd give to see her face when she spotted Jason, lying there like he was.

He should have stayed there. Waited for her. Killed her, too. After all, she had a part to play in all this. If she'd been a good wife, Jason wouldn't have had to find someone else to poke his dick into, would he.

Maybe I'll get her another day.

No 'maybe' about it. She had it coming to her. Soon.

He stopped at an all-night Sainsbury's garage, asking for some Butterkist through the intercom thing they used during the night at these places. He'd need it later. While he waited for the blonde female cashier to go and get the popcorn, his phone seemed to burn in his pocket. It contained the video of him with Jason. Interesting viewing wasn't the word. He'd watch it at some point when he had a moment.

"Three ninety-nine," the cashier said.

Was she having a laugh?

"What, for a bag that size?" he asked, something else burning in his other pocket. Cigar cutters.

No, don't use them here.

"That's garage prices for you, I'm afraid." She shrugged.

Her lack of care annoyed him, but not enough to do anything about it.

Lucky girl.

He paid, took his purchase out of the box in the wall she'd dropped it into, and got in his van. And spotted CCTV pointing right at his vehicle. Would the police check who was on the streets at this time of night once they found out Jason was dead? Check the *whole* city?

He'd fucked up.

Shit.

CHAPTER ONE

"Do you realise what a monumental fuck-up this is?" Bethany whispered to her partner, Mike, tapping her booted foot on the incident room floor, her mind racing with thoughts on how to fix this.

She glanced around at the other two members of her team, Leona and Fran. They were busy working, blonde heads bent, too far away to hear the conversation.

Good.

"What the hell am I going to tell the chief?" she said quietly.

"It's my fault, so I should be the one to tell him. I couldn't keep it from you any longer. The sleepless nights . . ." Mike scrubbed his black-bearded jaw. "I forgot to log it at the scene, all right? It happens. It got lost in the mountain of evidence, plus, I remember being distracted."

"But the case goes to bloody trial in the next few months." Bethany closed her eyes for a moment, calming herself so she didn't go off on one. "Actually, yes, you tell him, but I'll come with you. I won't let you do this alone. We stick together always, got it? First, though, we just need to think of an excuse as to *why* it wasn't logged."

"Um, because I forgot?"

"No, that's not how it happened, is it." She raised her eyebrows. "Do you get what I'm saying?"

"We lie?" *His* eyebrows lifted then.

I swear he plucks them.

"Er, yes?"

"Christ." He released a ragged breath. "What you're asking . . ."

"What I'm asking will save your arse. You could get a right old bollocking for this if you admit what you've done — or didn't do. And this lie isn't any different to the one you've been carrying around with you, is it?"

"What *do* I say then if I don't tell the truth?" The poor sod appeared fraught with indecision.

Catch twenty-two was a right arsehole.

She stared at a pile of papers on his desk. On the top was the piece of evidence Mike hadn't logged at the scene, sitting there all proud and alarming in its clear bag. The scrap of blood-soaked material inside had gone hard. It should have been with forensics, tested for type, DNA, not there in front of them.

It could still be done. They had time.

She rooted in his drawer for a pair of gloves and put them on. Then snatched up the bag and slid it down the side of his desk, between the solid panel leg and the wall.

"What are you doing?" Mike stared at her, his mouth hanging open.

"Take it back out." She held her breath, waiting for him to twig what she was up to.

"For fuck's sake. If I'm taking it back out, what was the point in putting it down there in the first place?"

"Take it back out!" *Keep your voice down, woman.*

Leona and Fran seemed oblivious, thank goodness.

"Damn," Bethany said. "I've just dropped your favourite pen down that slot." If she'd said it any louder, she'd have been shouting.

Mike pulled the desk away from the wall a bit so he could reach in and get the bag. He stood there holding it, and, Lord have mercy, dust and a cobweb clung to the surface. Nothing like authenticity.

His expression asked: *Now what?*

Bethany took the gloves off and stuffed them in her pocket. "Oh shit! Can you believe this? How the hell did *that* get down there?"

Mike didn't say a word.

"Must have slid off your desk at some point," Bethany went on. "Thank God you found it. This could massively help the Valiant case."

At last, realisation dawned. Mike nodded. "We need to get this to the chief."

"Too bloody right." Bethany winked and called out to Leona and Fran, "Look what's just turned up."

They swivelled in their seats.

"Only a piece of Valiant evidence." Bethany smiled. "It got wedged down the side of Mike's desk."

Leona scratched her head. "Will we get in trouble?"

"What, for an accident?" Bethany shook her head. "We all saw how many bags of evidence were on this desk back then." She tapped the wooden surface. "One was bound to go astray."

"But they get logged at the scene," Fran said, her forehead creasing. "Someone would have noticed it was missing by now."

"Well, with the amount of SOCO there, maybe it was forgotten. Maybe there was a slip up." *God forgive me for putting ideas in their heads and blaming it on someone else.* But there *had* been a tremendous amount of officers present. It *could* have happened this way. "Whoever found this bit of evidence put it in this bag here, and it's been written on, but shit happens, right? There are no initials as to who bagged it, though."

Miracles did happen.

Leona and Fran nodded.

"The main thing is, we have it now. Come on, Mike."

She led the way out and into the corridor. Mike stood beside her, and she looked up into his eyes once the door had closed. "I sounded plausible, yes?"

"Yes, but . . ."

"No buts."

"Does this make us bent coppers?" He stared down at the bag in his hand.

"Shut up with that sort of talk. It doesn't make us anything but liars. The keepers of a secret. The main thing is, we're fixing it now."

He nodded.

"It's not sitting right with you, is it?" she asked.

"No."

"Will possibly losing your job sit better? This will be the third thing on your sheet if you admit to what really happened. Why did you keep it quiet when you realised what you'd done?"

Mike shrugged. "Didn't want to admit I'd ballsed it up. Didn't want another mistake on my record."

"When did you actually find it?" She pointed to the bag.

"A week after I logged everything. Well, clearly not everything . . ."

A week would have been easier to deal with. Months had passed, so the course she'd now set in motion was the only way to smooth things over.

"Right, follow my lead." She walked down the corridor towards Chief Kribbs's office, glancing over her shoulder at Mike, who still stood there, forlorn and troubled. "Move your arse, Mike Wilkins, it's time to face the music."

* * *

"Thank heavens the phone saved us from one of his diatribes," Bethany said as they legged it downstairs to the car park after the meeting with Kribbs.

"I can't believe he swallowed the story." Mike's footfalls clattered on the steps behind her, relief evident in his voice.

"Yeah, well, I must have been convincing. Either that, or he has something more important rolling around in his noggin, so that was why he brushed it off. Be quiet now — people listen, add two and two together, and come up with the truth."

She shot out into reception. "Got that address for me?"

Rob Quarry, the front desk sergeant, held up a yellow Post-it note. "A bit of a mess there, by all accounts."

"Right. I don't want to be told before I see it for myself. What are we looking at as a charge?"

"Murder. His wife found him."

Bethany winced, putting herself in the woman's shoes. *Finding Vinny dead would just about kill me.* "Poor cow. Okay, we'll be going then." She took the note and handed it to Mike.

In the car, she set off fast, Mike still clipping in his belt.

"Fuck me, can you go any faster?" He gripped the 'oh shit' handle above the door.

"Prone to exaggeration much?" She laughed. "I drive fast, you know that. Get over it." To add the raspberry sauce and nuts on top of his crapping-his-pants Mr Whippy, she pressed her foot down harder.

"Not funny, Beth," he said.

She slowed. "Aww, where's your sense of humour?"

"I lost it when I messed up."

"Well, now it's fixed, so you can have a bit of a giggle again. I should have noticed something was wrong lately. You haven't been yourself. I just put it down to—"

"Don't even go there." He cleared his throat.

Mike's ex-girlfriend had been unable to cope with police hours and had left their shared home, only a Dear John letter propped on the mantelpiece to explain why she'd fucked off the cowardly way — to Dunnet Head in Scotland, no less. She couldn't have scarpered any farther. Apparently, she 'couldn't bear to see the upset' on Mike's face, hence the letter.

Bitch. I never did like her.

"Still raw then," she said. "You know, keeping it all inside isn't good for you. Talking it about it will help."

"I don't want to." He sighed.

"I'm here." She reached out and squeezed his knee. "I'm here."

"Maybe one day I'll open up."

"Make it soon, yes? I hate to see you like this. It's been six months." She turned left onto the housing estate renowned for residents with high-end everything. Rumour had it, even the women's fake toenails cost a fortune.

"I know how long it's been," Mike said. "Cheers for the reminder, though."

His comeback stung, and guilt settled inside her at her insensitivity. She'd come off as uncaring, and that was the last thing she wanted to do with Mike. They'd been partners for a long time. Years. "Shit, I didn't mean to rub it in. I want to help. I'm trying to, in my own clumsy way."

"I know. Ignore me." He ran a hand through his hair. "I'm just being a mardy arse."

"That you are. Anyway, we're here, look, so, as usual, personal stuff gets left inside the car as of now."

A SOCO van cuddled the kerb directly outside twenty-one Bladen Avenue, and the ME's red car, nudged up behind it, all but kissed its arse. The ME himself, Presley Zouch — named so on account of his mother being a tad too obsessed with Elvis, bless her blue-suede-shoe-loving heart — had once said, tongue in cheek, he'd chosen a red car because of the amount of blood he dealt with on a daily basis.

A twisted bastard, he was, but Bethany liked his bluntness. She knew where she stood with him.

She parked behind his Ford Ecosport and turned to Mike. "Ready, matey?"

"Yep. Let's get to it."

On the pavement, she scoped the area. Uniforms already stood at front doors — she made out Glen Underby and Nicola Eccles, her two favourite bobbies. "Nice to see our beloved front desk sergeant got the ball well and truly rolling. Rob's a godsend."

Mike nodded. "He certainly gets on with things."

She turned her attention to the property belonging to Jason and Georgia Holt. Mock Tudor, without the thatched roof. It had maybe five or six bedrooms, going by the amount of lead-paned windows. In the shingled front garden, potted plants and flowers bobbed in the slight breeze, which took the edge off the summer sun that seemed to have a mind to burn everything to a crisp this year. All in all, a pretty swanky place.

"Someone's got money," she said, idly wondering how much the council tax would be for a house that size.

"Doesn't everyone have it on this estate?"

"Hmm." She walked up the paved path slicing between the cream-coloured shingle and approached the officer at the front door.

Tory Yates handed over the log. Bethany signed it then passed it to Mike.

"Were you first on the scene?" she asked.

"No, Underby and Eccles." Tory grimaced. "I'm glad, because apparently, it isn't pleasant in there."

"Bugger." Bethany glanced at the box just inside the door. "Do we need full suits?"

"I'd say so." Tory grabbed a set each and held them out.

Bethany and Mike togged up on the doorstep, hoods in place, and Tory stepped aside to let them pass.

In the hallway, Bethany checked out their surroundings. Four doors off a large, square hallway. SOCOs were in the spacious kitchen to the right, swabbing blood that streaked the white worktops. Ahead, the door swung open, revealing dark wooden flooring, a cream leather sofa, and beside it, a mahogany occasional table with a blue vase full of flowers on top. The second door on the left had a SOCO kneeling under a desk — an office.

She turned to look at Tory's back. "Where's the wife?"

Tory spun round. "In there." She pointed to the closed door. "The dining room. It's been dusted and checked, given the all clear to use."

"Okay, thanks." Glancing at Mike, Bethany said, "Body or wife first?"

"Body." He sniffed. "We'll get a better sense of what she tells us if we know what she found first."

"True."

She led the way to the living room, assuming Jason's body was in there. Poking her head around the door, she sucked in a huge breath at the sight. Jason, in front of the fireplace. Blood everywhere, soaking into the rug, plastering the walls, stippling the mirror . . .

"Ah. I just need a second," she said and took a step back, staring at the floor to centre herself. Evidence markers sat beside blood scuffs in the hallway. Had the killer brought the blood out with them? Or had it been the wife? She stared up at Mike, who stood beside the table with the flowers.

"You okay, Beth?" he asked, eyes full of concern.

She steeled herself to go back inside. Nodded. "I have to be. I've got no choice."

CHAPTER TWO

Bethany stood a metre or so away from the body. The blood on the hardwood had long since dried, and photos had been taken, but she still felt bad for standing on what had once coursed through Jason's veins, even though a plastic sheet covered the area outside the rug.

Presley knelt beside Jason's legs, bending one to check for the status of rigor. Either Jason had been killed recently or rigor had come and gone. Going by the blood having dried, she'd say the latter.

Jason had been opened up like a tuna can, a circle of skin cut away, so big his whole midsection from below his ribs to his pelvis was exposed, an empty cavity. His innards had been removed, and his spine, covered in flesh and God knew what else, was the only thing left.

She switched her focus to his chest, and a piece of black material had been stuck to his skin, a white skull printed on it, staring at her as if it had seen exactly what had happened here, the eyes filling the sockets a disturbing shade of red. Skull images didn't usually have eyes, so what did that mean? And the fact the material had been *stuck* onto him . . . Had the killer known Jason would be alone for long enough to give them the opportunity to do this wicked thing? Or had they continued regardless and would have dealt with the wife if she'd come home in the middle of it?

Mike took a deep breath. "What the ever-loving fuck is this all about?"

"No idea. Was just wondering the same thing myself."

"I mean, his face . . ."

"I know."

Jason didn't have one, as such. His skin had been peeled off — cut again, same as his stomach — his muscles exposed, only a few yellow globules of fat clinging on. And his eyes . . . red contacts, a lock of his dark-brown fringe draping across one socket. Jason's smile no longer existed. Where his teeth were was anyone's guess.

"Do you think the skinning is significant?" she asked no one in particular. "That has to be a skill. Not everyone would know how to do that."

"Amazing what you can learn from Google," Mike said.

Presley stood, his ginger hair shining in the sunlight coming through the French doors. Blood stained his protective suit, almost perfect circles on the knees. "That's your area of expertise, finding significance." He took his pad out of his bag and drew, creating a picture of the body's position. "From what I can see, everything was done to him after death — the removal of skin, teeth, and innards. This would have taken quite a bit of time, so whoever did this knew he had a long window in which to carry out what they undoubtedly think of as their 'work'."

"I thought the same." Bethany sighed. "Any idea what time he died?"

"Rigor is on the cusp of being fully gone, so we're talking . . ." He checked the silver clock on the wall behind him. "It's three p.m. now, so I'll be generous and say between nine and midnight."

Isabelle Abbott, the lead SOCO, came to stand beside Bethany. "As you can imagine, with the wife finding him, she's buggered up the scene. The blood, as it presents here, isn't what it would have been had she not come in, so we've lost valuable information."

"I gather she stepped in it," Bethany said.

"Yes, which is why there's some in the hallway. She claims there wasn't any before that. She obviously missed the spots on the kitchen floor, maybe too tired to notice. She had no idea anything was wrong until she opened the door to this room."

"Okay. I'll go and speak to her now."

Bethany left and, with Mike following, knocked on the dining room door then entered. Georgia Holt, clad in pink pyjamas, sitting at a shiny mahogany table, looked up, her short blonde hair standing up all over the place, half her face covered in dried blood flecks. Alice Jacobs, the family liaison officer, sat beside her and widened her eyes at Bethany as if to say: *This is a tough person to deal with.* Giving a slight nod in thanks for the warning, Bethany approached the table and drew out a chair, as did Mike. They sat, and Bethany reached across to cover Georgia's bloodied hand with hers.

Thank goodness for gloves.

"I'm DI Bethany Smith, and this is my partner, DS Mike Wilkins. I'm in charge of this case, and first, I want to express my condolences."

Georgia stared, as though she wasn't all there.

Hardly surprising.

"Unfortunately, I'm going to have to ask you questions you may not feel like answering, but in order for us to find whoever did this, we need information. Do you understand?"

Georgia nodded.

"Okay. Let's start from last night. What time did you leave for work?"

Jason's wife seemed to compose herself, snapping out of whatever fugue she'd been in. "Eight-thirty, but I usually leave about nine."

"Did you notice whether anyone was outside?"

"No. I just went straight to my car."

"Then what?"

"I went to Sainsbury's. We needed a few bits and bobs."

"What did you buy?" Bethany didn't need to know, but if she could draw the woman out of the present and push her right into the past where she had to think, *properly* think about what she'd purchased, it might give her a few moments of respite, calming her before the real questions came.

"I . . . Baked beans, spaghetti, a loaf of Hovis. Thick cut. Jason likes it . . . Um . . ." She blinked and shook her head, clearly trying to think. "I have a receipt somewhere you can look at."

"I'd like you to tell me." She took her hand away.

Georgia closed her eyes. "I couldn't buy anything for the fridge or freezer as I was going straight to work after. Tomato sauce. Lindt chocolate, the orange bar. A BLT for my break. A small bottle of Coke. Beef Hula Hoops." She opened her eyes. "That's it, I think."

"Okay. What did you do after you'd been to Sainsbury's?"

"I used their garage. Filled the car up as Jason needs a full tank because he's going to . . .to his mother's for the weekend." She gasped. "Oh! Liz . . ."

"Liz is his mother?" Bethany tilted her head.

"Yes."

"Alice will deal with that for you now, if you like?"

Georgia nodded. "Liz lives in Cornwall." She slid her phone across the table. "Here, use that."

Alice picked it up and left the room.

"Where do you work?" Bethany asked.

"The hospital."

"Here, in Shadwell?"

"Yes."

"And what do you do there?"

"I'm a nurse in A and E."

"What time did you finish?"

"Time ran over. It usually does. I should have been done about eight this morning, but I finally got out around ten."

Bethany wondered why Alice felt Georgia was a difficult person to deal with. Maybe the poor woman hadn't wanted to speak until now. "Where did you go then?"

"I drove straight here and went to bed. Jason was supposed to be at work today, so I didn't go and check his office to say hello — he sometimes works from home."

"How long did you sleep for?"

"I climbed in bed about half ten but woke with stomach pain. I got up at twelve-fifteen and went downstairs to get some Andrews. I made a cup of tea. Filled a hot water bottle. I was going to sit and watch TV on the sofa under a blanket until I fell asleep again but . . ." Tears fell down her cheeks. "I . . ." She swallowed. "I saw him there, recognised his clothes, and, well, I rushed over to see if I could resuscitate him. I registered the state of his stomach, his face, but I tried anyway. Stupid of me."

"I can understand why you did that. It's hope, isn't it?"

"It was. Even though I knew . . ." She blew out a breath. "I pumped his chest, then went to give mouth-to-mouth but didn't . . . It was useless. So I-I pressed my cheek to his and . . ." She lifted a hand to the blood-flecked side of her face. "And I cuddled him."

Bethany took in the fact Georgia had red stains on her pyjama top. The poor woman had been distraught, her nurse training fleeing her head when it had come to someone she loved. While the crime scene had been tampered with, she empathised with Georgia's reaction.

Could I think about scene preservation if I found Vinny like that?

She shoved thoughts of her husband from her mind. "What happened then?"

"I rang the police." Her bottom lip wobbled.

"Okay, this is where—"

Alice returned and sat beside Georgia. "Your mother-in-law will be here as soon as she can. You'll have to stay at a hotel — I'll sort that for you — as the house is now a—"

"I understand." Georgia nodded. "I'm worried about her driving when she's had this sort of news. She's . . . like a mum to me, too. Mine's dead."

"It's all right. Jason's brother is coming with her." Alice patted Georgia's shoulder.

Georgia sighed out her relief.

"Right." Bethany had to get things rolling again. "This is where the questions may be upsetting, but I have to ask them. Do you know of anyone who would have wanted to do this to Jason?"

Georgia wiped her eyes, smearing some of the dried blood with her tears. "He runs his own construction company. There have been a few people upset over the years, but Jason always resolved issues, fixing whatever they weren't happy with, free of charge. I can't imagine any of them would want to kill him."

"What's the name of the company?"

"JJ Builders."

"What does the second J stand for?"

"Junior. His dad was also called Jason. His business cards are in his office. For the address," Georgia said.

Bethany wouldn't press for her to repeat the information herself. "Thank you. We'll need to question his employees. Has he ever fallen out with any of them in the past?"

"No, they're a great bunch."

"Good. Think back to Jason's earlier years. Is there anything there that means someone might hold a grudge?"

"Not that I know of. Liz might, though." She laced her fingers on the table.

"What kind of person was Jason?" Bethany waited for the usual: lovely, wouldn't hurt anyone, a good person.

"He's got a temper, and I'm wondering if he annoyed the wrong person that's nothing to do with business."

Bethany raised her eyebrows. "A temper? In what way?"

"He has a short fuse. He isn't a mean man, just that he flies off the handle from time to time." Georgia bit her lip. "Think of it as a kid stamping his feet if he doesn't get his own way. Once he's calmed down, he's back to normal again. It doesn't make him any less loveable."

"So he was fine in all respects apart from that?"

She hesitated for a bit too long. "Yes."

"Where was he when you left for work last night?"

"In his home office. I went in there to say goodbye, but he didn't speak to me as he was on the phone, so he just waved, and I blew him a kiss." She shut her eyes briefly at that.

"Did you speak to him on the phone at all during your shift or have any other form of contact?"

"No."

"Is he on social media?"

"Yes, and I run his work pages."

Bethany's heart skipped a beat. "So you have the passwords for each account?"

"Yes. Twitter and Facebook."

"We'll need those and the email addresses you log in with. His computer will be taken away, but you can have it back once we're finished," Mike said.

Bethany had all but forgotten he was sitting there. He slid his notebook across the table along with a pen. Georgia wrote the details down then pushed it back. She'd also added Jason's work address and two mobile numbers, so that would save having to go into the office to get his card.

"Why two mobiles?" Bethany asked. "Work and personal?"

"Yes."

"What was his social life like?" Bethany needed a picture of him outside the home, other than for his job.

"He doesn't have one."

"What about you as a couple?"

"We don't really have time, and to be honest, I'm always too tired to go out."

All through this, Georgia had spoken in the present tense about Jason. Although she'd seen her husband's corpse, it hadn't sunk in yet that he was dead. Maybe because he didn't resemble what he'd looked like in life. A thought struck her then, and she'd have to ask the hardest question of all.

"Are you sure the body is Jason's?"

Georgia's eyes filled, and she nodded. "Yes. He has a tattoo on his wrist. An eagle. I checked — it was there."

"We might need to come and speak to you again at some point, but for now, we must get on. Thank you for your time."

Bethany and Mike left the room.

"Quick tour of the house?" she asked Mike.

He nodded, and they climbed the stairs. At the top, a SOCO knelt on the large bathroom floor, swabbing beside the bath.

"Sorry to disturb you," Bethany said. "Have you got something there?"

He nodded and popped the swabber in a plastic tube. "Looks like blood to me." He peered over the bath. "If you come and look, there's faint traces in there, too. We've already used the light on it — definitely blood present."

"So the cheeky bastard had a shower here?" Bethany widened her eyes.

"Seems so," the SOCO said. "I mean, they'd have been covered in the red stuff, so leaving here dirty would have drawn attention."

"Depending on what time they left."

"Hmm." He went back to his task.

Bethany and Mike checked all the bedrooms — five; four spares and one belonging to the couple. All were tidy apart from theirs — an unmade bed, Georgia's nurse's uniform thrown on a chair, curtains drawn, the en suite blind down. A couple of SOCOs dusted for fingerprints.

Back downstairs, they returned to the living room. Presley had gone, but Isabelle Abbott was still there.

"Ah, Beth," she said. "Presley asked me to tell you he'll let you know the cause of death tomorrow. There was nothing obvious he could see today."

"Okay, thanks. What are your thoughts?"

"What, on cause of death?"

"Well, any of this." Bethany gestured to the room in general.

"If you look at the hearth, each front corner has a decorative brass ball with a spike. See the one farthest from you? I'd say he hit his head on it, so perhaps there was a struggle. We could be talking intruder, which led to murder, although why they took parts of him away, I don't know."

Neither did Bethany, but it was now time to find out.

She did the official walk-through of the house with Isabelle, who pointed out various things Bethany had missed before — blood smudges that hadn't been washed off in the bathroom, spots of blood on the kitchen floor, which had dropped from a height, indicating Jason had possibly been injured in there first — then she left with Mike to go to JJ Builders.

CHAPTER THREE

"What the fuck do you want?" Jason asked, staring through the gap at the front door.

God, this bloke was such an arrogant bastard.

"I need to talk to you," T said.

"What about?" Jason's eyes narrowed.

"You really want to do this on the doorstep when Georgia could come home at any second? She could have forgotten something. Or I could have rung her to make her come back . . ."

"Look, we sorted this. You shouldn't be here." Jason shook his head.

"Doesn't matter whether you think I should be. I'm here now. Unless you want me to shout it all out in the street, you'll let me inside. I hear Georgia's quite pally with the next-door neighbour. Heidi, isn't it? Would you like Heidi to know what you've done? I'm sure she'd give that nugget of info to Georgia."

"For fuck's sake." Jason's famous temper was showing. He clenched his fist, his face going red.

How amusing.

Jason opened the door farther and led the way to his office. He flopped into his chair. "So, what's left to say? We said it already."

"No, we didn't. Or rather, you *didn't."*

"What do you mean? I accepted I fucked—"

"Yeah, you fucked all right, and that's what all this mess is about, isn't it."

"I was going to say fucked up."

"That and all. But you didn't say sorry, did you. And I've been waiting all this time for an apology to come — it's ages since I told you what you'd done, isn't it? — but here I am, still without one."

"Sorry? Why do I need to say sorry to you?"

"Because she was my sister."

"What?" Jason reared his head back in shock. "You didn't say that before. All you told me was she needed money for a private abortion. I didn't know—"

"Who the hell did you think I was then?"

"A friend."

"A friend. Right. Don't you even care that she died?"

"She died?"

"I texted and told you about it."

Jason shook his head, shock twisting his face. "I changed my phone number because she kept ringing me. Georgia would have found out. I couldn't risk it."

"Yeah, she died. In some shitty abortion clinic — some complication with her heart. She died because you got her pregnant, and if you hadn't, she wouldn't have had to get rid of it, so in my book, that's your fault. I put her in the ground last week. I can't afford to pay for the rest of the instalments to the funeral home so I'm here to collect. The least you can do is fork out for her send-off."

"I can't just give you a few grand. Georgia does my books for me. She'll notice the withdrawal."

"Don't you go thinking I'm daft. I know about the money in your safe at work. My sister told me all about it. Wasn't that where you shagged her? In your office?"

Jason closed his eyes.

"You're going to go there. Now. You'll get the money, then you'll come back. I'll wait. If you don't *come back, I'll be right here for when your wife arrives in the morning."*

"You piece of shit wanker." Jason pushed up out of his chair and grabbed a set of keys off his desk. "If you roll up here again after this, I swear I'll . . ."

"You swear you'll what?"

"Nothing. Sit there and don't move." Jason pointed to his seat.

"You're not really in a position to tell me what to do, are you?"

Jason stormed out, and a few seconds later, the front door slammed shut.

What a twat.

T wandered around the house, checking all the rooms for something small he could steal and use later, just for kicks. Georgia's jewellery. A couple of those posh Swarovski crystals — a swan, a teardrop. All those things brought back a memory he'd rather forget, and he felt sick that fate had played her hand and shown them to him, all at the same time. He swallowed down anger and shoved them in his pocket without looking at them, and by the time he returned downstairs, Jason stood in the hallway.

He held a wedge of money and thrust it at him. "Take it and piss off. No more."

"I'll need a bag."

Jason stomped off to the kitchen and pulled a plastic carrier out of a caddy under the sink. "Here."

T took it and dropped the cash inside. "Did you love her?"

Jason laughed. "Did I fuck. She was just some piece of skirt."

That didn't go down too well. He reached over to the knife block and pulled out the longest one. The blade was buried in Jason's stomach inside three seconds. He thought about his sister's red eyes when he'd seen her in the morgue, where she'd had some kind of haemorrhage and they'd turned scarlet. He thought about her face, which had looked skeletal, a skull with thin skin on top. And he thought about her insides, minus the baby she'd been too frightened to keep because their dad would have gone crazy at her for getting pregnant.

Everything was in his backpack in the van, ready for just this moment. He'd planned it all, right down to skinning Jason's face for the significance of his sister's being skull-like, for how it related to his lovely Chelsea.

Jason stared down at the knife, then back up at him. "What the . . . ?"

"She was fifteen, you fucking pervert."

"Don't you think I know that?"

"You knew?" Anger boiled. "My mum's broken." Good, she deserves to be. *"I reckon your mum ought to suffer the same, don't you?"*

"No, no, please . . ."

"Shut up, you nonce twat. It's time you paid the real *price."*

CHAPTER FOUR

Bethany and Mike stood outside a Portakabin in the yard. A sign with JJ Builders had been attached above one of the windows, and she peered inside. It looked like a staff room. Formica-topped tables, black plastic chairs, a sink unit, the drainer covered in upside-down cups, and two vending machines, one for snacks, one for drinks. Oh, and a white kettle that was too grubby for words.

"Can I help you?" Male. Sounded like he'd been shouting and his voice had gone hoarse.

Bethany spun round and faced him. "DI Bethany Smith and DS Mike Wilkins." She took her ID out and held it up, then slid it into her back pocket.

His yellow hard hat pressed down on shoulder-length black hair, and his tan gave away the fact that he worked outdoors. He had no top on, showing off his bulging muscles, and dust clung to his skin. A tool belt hung off his waist, a hammer sticking out of one of the pockets. He must be boiling in those skinny jeans and big boots.

"You finally found whoever it is robbing the store shed then?" he asked, cocking a craggy eyebrow.

He reminded her of a younger version of her dad.

“Um, no. That wouldn’t necessarily be something we’d deal with. I need to speak to all of Mr Holt’s employees. Would that be possible?”

“I should say so. They’ll all be turning up shortly.” He glanced at his watch. “Yep, five minutes or so. They’re out on jobs but have to come back here to clock off. What do you need to speak to them for?”

She stared around the courtyard. A bungalow that might have been someone’s home once upon a time stood to the right. “Is that Jason’s office?”

“Yep, although he only uses one of the rooms for that. The rest is done out like a normal home. His mum and brother stay in it when they come up this way.”

“I see. Do you have a key?”

“No, that I don’t have, but I do have one for the Portakabin. You can talk to the workers in there if you like. You didn’t answer me before. Why d’you need to speak to them?”

“You as well, but it’s best I say what’s happening one to one.” She smiled, peering over his shoulder at a large white van turning into the yard. “What’s your name?”

“Sam King.”

“Okay, Sam, I’ll need you to stay out here and make sure all the other employees hang around.”

“No more will turn up,” Sam said. “They’re all in the back of that van. They get dropped off at each location, then picked up again.”

It sounded like a well-run company.

“Okay. I’ll need that Portakabin opened up, then I’ll speak to whoever wants to go first.”

Once Sam unlocked the door, she got the interviews underway, asking them all not to say what had happened to Jason to any of the others as they left. With Sam the last to come in, she could finally put the poor bloke out of his misery.

He sat at the table opposite Bethany and Mike. “What the shit is going on? Everyone came out of here with a face like a slapped arse.”

"I'll get to that in a moment." Tired down to her bones, and with it being way past six now, Bethany pushed herself to go through it all again. "What's your role here, Mr King?"

"I'm the supervisor. I have my own van, and I drive round to all the locations daily to make sure everything's going smoothly."

"Okay. How well do you know Mr Holt?"

"We're mates. Been hanging around with each other since secondary school. Why are you asking me about him?"

"Good mates, are you?"

"I'd say so. Look, no offence, like, but this is pissing me off. Can't you just get to the point?"

"Just answer my questions, Mr King. Do you know of anyone who'd want to harm Mr Holt?"

"Jason? He's got himself into bother with that big gob of his before now, but nothing that warrants him being hurt. Well, no more than a punch on the nose."

"What sort of bother?"

"He was a loud mouth when he was younger. Liked having fights in the pub of a Friday and Saturday night, the usual thing from a bloke in his twenties. Then he met Georgia, and that calmed him down. Now he just gets on with work and goes home."

"Did he tell you he wouldn't be in for work today?"

"Nope, but then he doesn't have to, really, does he, what with being the boss. If he's in, he's in. If he isn't, none of my business, and besides, I can always give him a ring if I need to. He leaves the running of this place to me most of the time. Pays me well for it, too."

"Did you try calling him today?"

Sam shook his head. "Wasn't any need. Things were going along fine."

"Did you ring him last night, just before eight-thirty?"

"I did as it happens. I asked if he wanted to go out for a bevvy — my wife had gone to bingo with her mates — but he said no. We chatted for a bit, and he said he had to go as Georgia had just left for work and he wanted to chill out and watch a bit of telly. 'Ere, hang on a minute . . . you just asked if anyone would want to harm Jason. Is that why everyone else looked a bit shaken up? Has something happened?"

Deciding Sam didn't appear or sound dodgy, Bethany said, "I'm afraid Mr Holt was murdered last night."

"You fucking what?" Sam blinked a fair few times, and his mouth gaped. "Jason? Murdered? Who the hell would want to do that?"

"Maybe for money?"

"Well, he's worth a bob or two, but . . ." Sam wiped his brow. "Sorry, but I can't get my head around this. He's my *mate*."

"I'm sorry to have given you such distressing news. Now, one of the other workers — and no, I won't say who it was — mentioned Jason having a young woman in his office from time to time. Know anything about that?"

Sam's cheeks turned red. "Ah, keep me out of that bollocks. I'm not getting involved. Like I told him when he was shagging her, she looked too young, and what with me knowing Georgia, it didn't sit right."

"So he was having an affair?"

"I don't know that it was a proper affair, but if a girl's in there, your guess is probably the same as mine."

"Do you know her name?"

"Nope, and I don't want to." He scrubbed at his chin. "I had a go at him — Jason — told him he shouldn't be playing around. Georgia's a lovely woman — she's friends with my wife."

"Did you tell your wife what Mr Holt was up to? Or what you suspected he was doing?"

He shook his head. "I wanted to — we share everything, me and Liv — but I knew she'd tell Georgia, and I couldn't stand for her to be upset. She doesn't deserve him cheating on her."

"Do you know if the relationship is still ongoing — with the other woman?"

"He said he finished it a month or so back. I know he had to get a new phone because she kept ringing him, and he was well worried Georgia would find out, although why he gave the bit on the side his number is beyond me. So he told Georgia he'd lost his mobile on a building site, you know, to cover up." He sighed. "Christ, this is just horrible. How did he . . . ? What did they do to him?"

"You really don't want to know. Now, if you could just give us your address and phone number . . ."

With that written down, Bethany and Mike said their goodbyes and left the Portakabin. They got in the car, and Bethany stared at the 'office'.

"We'll have to get keys for that place. It needs looking at." She rang Isabelle. "Are you still at the Holt's?"

"I am, unfortunately."

"We're at JJ buildings, Jason's company. There's a bungalow here that he uses as an office and somewhere for his mother to stay. He's been playing away, if you catch my drift. Been taking a young woman there. Thing is, we have no keys, so if you could ask Georgia for them . . ."

"She's gone to The Ringer Hotel to wait for Jason's mother and brother. I can have a look for them. I'm guessing you need SOCO down there?"

"Yes, to be on the safe side. There might be something inside we can use to help us."

"Okay, leave that with me."

"Thanks." She cut the call and lowered the window. "Sam?" she called as he left the Portakabin and locked it.

He came over. "Yep?" It appeared he'd been crying, the poor sod.

"Do you still have Jason's old number?"

He took his phone out of his pocket, scrolled through it, then turned the screen to face her. She reeled it off to Mike, who wrote it down.

"Thank you. Just another quick question. What did the young girl look like?"

"Blonde, skinny, big tits. Her face is a bit like Sharon's from *Eastenders*."

"Okay, thanks again. If we need you, we'll be in touch."

He nodded and walked over to a small red van.

"Come on," she said to Mike. "I'll drop you home."

"Cheers. I'll just ring this number in. They can get someone checking into it, ask for the records or whatever."

"Good thinking."

Once he'd done that, she asked him to call Leona at the station to find out if they'd found anything yet. They hadn't, so he told them to pack up for the day.

She took Mike to his house, waved at his black cat sitting on the windowsill in the living room, then drove home. Vinny's car was in the drive, and she smiled. Parking next to it, she gathered what strength she had left and entered the house. The scent of fish and chips wafted down the hallway, so she walked into the kitchen. Vinny sat at the table sprinkling salt on his food.

"Hi, love," she said. "Have a good day?"

He scrunched up his blond eyebrows. "If you can call not getting to a fire in time to save the occupant a good day . . ."

"Oh shit, I'm sorry." She went over and hugged him.

"It was an old lady. She was stuck in her bloody wheelchair."

Bethany closed her eyes. How he did his job, she didn't know. Then again, he didn't know how she did hers. She'd met him at a charity auction, where various emergency services personnel were raising money. With them both understanding how hours in their jobs weren't the usual nine-to-five, they'd gone into the relationship knowing all the pitfalls. So far, it had worked well, but Vinny took deaths to heart, couldn't switch off, and he'd be down for days now.

"I've left your dinner in the packet," he said.

"Thanks."

She dished it up — he'd bought her a chicken and mushroom Pukka pie, chips, and a pot of gravy, God love him. They were still hot, so she sat at the table opposite him to enjoy a meal that wasn't hours old and needed microwaving, for once. He asked about her day.

"You don't want to know," she said, then shoved a chip in her mouth. "It's grisly and upsetting, and we haven't got the faintest idea why he was killed."

"Rather you than me."

They finished their meals in silence, Vinny probably reliving the fire, Bethany walking through the crime scene in her head, solidifying the layout, what she'd seen, and what Georgia had said. She churned it all around in her mind, then thought about the interviews with Jason's staff. All of them thought highly of him. He was a fair boss who paid well. Nice bloke, if a bit bad-tempered at times. So who would have wanted him dead? If Sam was to be believed and the woman Jason had been having sex with was young, had someone got the hump about their relationship?

Depends on how young . . .

She shuddered at that thought, but it was something to consider, especially since Sam had mentioned it. She should have asked him what age he thought she was — younger than eighteen didn't mean a thing if she was over sixteen.

Dinner done with, she went and had a bath. Unless a call came in, she was going to put this out of her head until the morning. She could compartmentalise and wished Vinny was the same way. Unfortunately, when she went down to the living room in her pyjamas, he was sitting on the sofa with a beer in hand, his face a sad mask. She sat beside him and held his hand while they both stared at the blank TV screen.

"I love you," she said, thinking of Georgia without Jason now.

"I know," he said. "Let's watch a film, shall we?"

Bless him. He was making an effort to cheer up.

God, she really did love him, just like she'd said.

CHAPTER FIVE

"Hello?"

"Good afternoon. I'm calling from Bishway Solutions, and I'd like to offer you a free trial for justice served—"

"Who?"

"Bishway Solutions."

"Is this one of those bloody cold calls?"

"Mr Holt, please listen a moment while I run you through your options—"

"How did you get my fucking name?"

How indeed.

"If you could just give me five minutes of your time, I—"

"Haven't you got anything better to do than phone people up, bugging them to—"

"Haven't you got anything better to do than having an affair?"

Ooh, cold. So cold.

"Who the hell is this?" Jason snapped.

"I've told you. I'm from Bishway Solutions, where justice is served."

"Look, you need to fuck right off."

"No, you look. You need to watch your back." He slammed the handset down on his old-fashioned green phone and laughed.

Then laughed some more.

* * *

"Hello?" Opal said.

"Good morning. I'm calling from Bishway Solutions, and I'd like to offer you a free trial for justice served—"

"Sorry, I don't take cold calls."

"You might want to take this one."

"Excuse me?"

"How does it feel to have killed someone while you're in the process of removing their baby?" That had to have hurt her. He almost giggled.

"Who is this?"

"Answer me. How does it feel?"

"How did you get my number?"

"How did you get away with it?"

She ended the call.

"Bitch." He rang her again.

"Hello?"

"Good morning. I'm calling from Bishway Solutions—"

Dialling tone.

More laughter. So. Much. More.

* * *

"Go and check your sister, T." Dad always called him that, and it had stuck. Now everyone did it.

T walked off down the street to the park at the end. Chelsea loved going there, whooshing back and forth on the swings. She'd stay for hours if she could. She'd gone with her little friend, the pair of them seven, and with T being older at sixteen, it was his job to go and make sure she was okay every so often. Ever since she'd been born, T had taken it upon himself to watch out for her. Dad might be nasty to him, but T vowed he wouldn't let him treat Chelsea the same way. T took the blame for everything she did, just so she wouldn't get a smack.

Or worse.

Mum was a useless piece of shit, always in bed all day. He hated her.

He walked down the road and waited at the entrance to the park. There Chelsea was, swinging away, hair flying, squealing every time she went too high. Her little mate, Nat, was on the roundabout, getting all dizzy and shit.

T returned home. "She's fine."

"She can have ten more minutes, then go and get her."

T had planned to go out with Stevie in a sec, but his sister came first, always would. He texted Stevie: GOING TO BE A BIT LATE. SOZ.

With Chelsea's time up, T went back to the park. She was having so much fun, he didn't want to make her go home, but Dad would go off on one, and that was the last thing either of them needed.

She put her tiny hand in his, and Nat did the same on his other side. He dropped Nat off at her house first, and her mother thanked him and called him 'such a good lad'. He smiled and waved, then took Chelsea home, her skipping beside him, and wasn't that just great to see? She had no worries in this moment, and she looked up at him with a gappy grin.

His heart hurt as he stared back at her.

He loved her so much.

He'd do anything for her.

Anything.

* * *

T accessed the video on his phone, standing at his bedroom window, the light off, only the illumination from the screen giving a soft glow. With the curtains open, anyone could peer up and catch sight of him, and although they wouldn't see much, *he'd* know he was stark naked.

He got a thrill from that.

Pressing PLAY, he remembered propping the phone up on the sideboard in the living room at Jason's house after he'd dragged him in there from the kitchen. The blood hadn't been flowing freely at that point, what with the knife still sticking out of him, and T had been glad about that. He'd wanted Georgia to have no clues that would alert her to what she'd find.

Surprise was sometimes a frightening thing.

The image on screen wobbled as T had put the phone in place, wanting the right angle. Jason stood in front of the cream fluffy rug, the fireplace behind him, the back of his head reflected in the mirror.

T busted out the Butterkist, settling down to watch and remember.

* * *

"Please," Jason said. "We can work something out."

"Whatever we do, it isn't going to bring Chelsea back, is it?"

"No, but I swear, I didn't mean for anything like this to happen. Like I told you, I didn't even know she was dead."

"You thought she'd scuttled off like a good little kid, didn't you?" T shook his head. "You thought she'd got the message when you didn't answer your phone and didn't open the door to your 'office'. Office, my arse. It's got a bedroom. A kitchen, just like a real house."

Jason closed his eyes and winced. Probably in pain.

Good.

"Hurt, does it?" T asked, walking into shot.

"Please, call an ambulance. I need them to get this thing out of me."

"What, like this?" T reached forward and pulled the knife out.

Blood gushed.

"Oh fuck, oh fuck . . ." Jason stared down at his stomach then clutched the wound.

"I'm going to make that hole bigger in a minute," T said.

"Fuck off now. Just go. You've made your point." Jason moved towards him, his eyes narrowed, his features skewing with anger.

T couldn't let him pass. Couldn't let him get hold of a phone to ring for help — or to leave the house and find it. He punched Jason, who went down, landing half on the hearth, cracking his head on one of those brass balls with a spike on top.

So it seemed he was dead, then. A bit of a bummer that. T had wanted to slit his throat. Still, the job was done — the killing part anyway — and now it was time to do the rest.

T got on with it, using his tools on the stomach, and it was a harder job than he'd thought it would be. Skinning his face wasn't, though. T had learnt how to do that with rabbits, and, granted, a human face was tougher to work on, but he'd done it in the end. Jason's face looked just like a skeleton now, same as Chelsea's had.

He put red contacts on the eyes, then got out his skull picture and used Superglue to attach it to the chest — he'd had to clean a space so it wasn't wet with blood. Why didn't anyone tell you killing had some inconvenient aspects to it?

* * *

The screen went blank. T shoved a handful of popcorn in his mouth and chewed. The silly cow at the garage had given him the salty kind. He preferred toffee. He might have to visit her again and have a go at her about it.

* * *

Once he'd done everything he'd set out to do, he put all the innards and skin into a large container and placed it by the door. In the far corner where it was clean, he put his pay-as-you-go phone and the knife in an inner pocket of his bag, then pulled a plastic jumpsuit out. With it on over his drenched clothes, at the living room doorway, he covered his boots in carrier bags, tying them on with the handles, and stepped over the threshold one foot at a time so no blood got out there.

Off upstairs he went to the bathroom, getting smears of blood here and there as he removed his clothes, stuffing all the red-coated stuff into a black sack. Clean after a shower, he left the water running and stepped out to scrub the scarlet off the floor, sink, walls, and door where he'd accidentally brushed against them. Back beneath the spray, he washed until he was sure every speck was gone from his hair and skin. He dumped the black bag in the bath while he dried himself on a navy-blue towel, then hauled the towel and the bag downstairs.

He dressed in the clean corner in fresh clothes, leaving the house shortly afterwards, feet bare, storing his bags and the box in the back of the van. At home, he burnt the clothing and towel on the barbecue, laughing to himself, telling Chelsea's ghost he was making everything as right as he could, although totally right would be having her still alive.

Like Dad said, you couldn't have everything.

He drove away again, down to the river, dropping the box and cleaned knife inside a bag into the water, then rang that silly cow at the emergency services.

All in all, it had been a good night's work.

Except for his stupid trip to the garage and seeing that bloody CCTV camera.

* * *

Butterkist all gone, reminiscing done, T got up and walked to his green landline phone.

He dialled the abortion bitch.

"Hello?"

"Good evening. I'm calling from Bishway Solutions, and I'd like to offer you a free trial—"

"Listen, you," she snarled, her voice shaking. "I'm going to dial one-four-seven-one or whatever the hell it is and get your number and report you."

"Good luck with that."

"You've withheld it, haven't you? Well, BT can still do something about it. I'll—"

"What you're going to do is shut your fucking mouth and listen to me."

"I'm calling the police. You—"

"Do you love your mum?"

"What?"

"I said, do you love your mum?"

"What's this got to do with . . . No. Oh no. Please don't do that."

"Do what?"

"Threaten her."

"Who said anything about threatening her? Killing is better, don't you think?"

"What do you want from me?" she wailed.

"You'll see."

He lowered the cradle onto the phone and, as usual, laughed.

CHAPTER SIX

Opal put the phone down, scared to death. Whoever kept calling her clearly knew she was the one who'd performed the operation on Chelsea Bishway. It had unfortunately made the news, and reporters had camped out in her street, waiting to get a glimpse of her as she left for work, especially on the day of the burial.

The death hadn't been her fault, but try telling the journalists that, or the people who gave her funny looks since her face had been splashed in the online newspapers, the local rags, too. Seeing herself on the front page of *The Shadwell Herald* in the little shop down the road had given her a nightmare.

She'd just been doing her job, and an unforeseen problem with Chelsea's heart had meant she'd died on the table. The poor girl had been too far along in her pregnancy to go down a different route, which would be having a suppository instead of an operation. It was all getting a bit too much — the guilt, remorse, and fear.

Opal rang her mother, just to be sure she was okay. She was fine, she said, so Opal made up some cock and bull story that she wanted to check because of the press possibly going round there to bug her mum next.

You'll see. That was what he'd said to her.

She'd see what he wanted from her. When, though? Would he leave her waiting and wondering until she went mad from it?

Her stomach rolled. Living on this knife edge since the death had wreaked havoc on her nerves. The fact that Chelsea had been fifteen didn't help matters, although Opal hadn't known that at the time of the operation. Someone else dealt with that side of things, and Chelsea had appeared much older. It turned out she'd used fake ID. How did that even happen? How did it get past those higher up in the chain than Opal?

She'd thought working in a private clinic would be better than the NHS, but it just went to show that it didn't matter where she was employed. If things went wrong, word spread.

Had some crackpot been following the news and decided to pick on her? Or was it someone from Chelsea's family? She didn't know, but whoever it was had it in for her, big-time. What were they going to do to her? Continue to harass? Ask for money? She had a bit stashed away in a savings account, but would it be enough to keep this man happy?

It was the thing he'd said about serving justice that got her the most. So he wanted her to pay, did he? Hadn't she paid enough with culpability? Her face in the news? Everyone around here knowing exactly who she was, giving her the cold shoulder now? Even her friends had backed off.

Some friends they were.

She sighed and got ready for bed, then sank beneath the covers, shivering, waiting for her phone to ring again. He'd taken to calling her at all times, no pattern, so she never knew when the bloody thing would jingle. It resulted in a lack of sleep, leaving her jittery and caffeined up to the eyeballs just to get through the day.

Maybe she should move away. Start again. Change her name, too. Study for a new career. Something, anything other than this horrible life she lived now. Some would say it was better than having no life, like Chelsea, but right at this minute, Opal would switch places with her.

Her eyelids drooped, and she drifted towards sleep, focusing on her breathing and not her thoughts. Her body grew heavy, as though an unseen hand pulled her through the mattress by her pyjama top, and she let it tug, let it take over.

Sleep. Blessed oblivion.

* * *

Opal listened to a lullaby, the voice singing it male, but light and soothing in tone.

Creepy.

The hairs on the back of her neck rose.

"Hush little baby don't say a word, T's gonna make sure you feel the hurt . . ."

That wasn't right, was it?

She frowned.

"And if that hurt don't make you cry, T's gonna make sure you tell him why."

She froze at hot breath ghosting over her left cheek. Scrunched her eyes tight, her heart hammering. Someone was on her bed, beside her. She sensed that now — the way the mattress slanted slightly beneath her, to the left. The heat of a body, close, too close. An invasion of space and privacy. The sound of air going in and out of them — and her.

"And before this wretched night pans out, T's gonna make you scream and shout."

She made to shoot up, but something held her down — an arm across her collarbone? Opal parted her lips to scream, just like he'd said she would, but a hand clamped over her mouth, and the person shifted from next to her and sat on top, a heavy weight on her chest, her arms pinned by his knees.

She struggled to breathe. To think.

"And now the time has come to pay, T's gonna make sure you go away."

No. No!

She thrashed beneath him, bucking her arse to try to shove him off. When that didn't work, she kicked, but he was too far up her body, and her legs and feet landed nowhere except mid-air and the mattress.

He reached over to the nightstand and put her lamp on. Then stared down at her.

A replica of Chelsea in male form. Blond hair. Thick eyebrows. Cupid's-bow lips.

"Good evening. Or morning now. The early hours," he said conversationally, as if he really was one of those cold callers. "I'm from Bishway Solutions, and I'd like to offer you death."

A scream rose from inside her but couldn't get out past his hand. It remained lodged in her throat, a hoarse groan, and she thought her heart might give out on her it beat so fast. She pissed herself, fear careening through her, and oddly, embarrassment for the accident, too.

He leant across and lifted a sock from the bed then shoved it into her mouth. She gagged, eyes watering, and attempted to speak, to tell him there must be something she could do that would stop this . . . *This.*

He picked up a length of rope from her right-hand side and drew one of her arms out, then the other, gripping her hands together in one of his large ones. She fought anew, hoping to scratch his face, but he was too strong and had her wrists bound in no time. With them secured to one of the poles of her headboard, she was up shit creek.

The man got off her, swiped up more rope, and walked to the end of the bed. "On the phone, I said, 'You'll see.'" A pause. "Do you see *now*?"

Yes, she saw all right, but what was he going to do next? She remembered his weird lullaby and what he'd said afterwards. Hurt. Making her go away.

Death.

Ohfuckohfuckohfuck.

She kicked, stretching her legs to hit him with her feet, but she was too short. He laughed, revealing long teeth.

She wore herself out with the kicking, terror rendering her motionless now. He closed his lips and just stood there staring at her, a predatory gleam in his mad eyes.

"And if you don't go away too quick, T's gonna bash your head with a brick." He laughed again, maniacally, for too long.

So long she sobbed, hating the sound, wishing it would stop.

"I'm joking." He sobered, glaring. "I have a hammer."

* * *

"What's your emergency?"

"I killed a woman."

"Where?"

"In her house."

"Sir, where is that?"

"In her street."

"What's your name, sir?"

"Fuck off."

CHAPTER SEVEN

Bethany and Mike stood in the car park at the station. The sun was out in force again, far too warm for seven forty-five in the morning. It was going to be another sweltering day, and Bethany wanted nothing more than to lounge at home in her back garden, but there was a killer to catch and, good weather or not, she had to help find him or her, preferably before the moon made another appearance.

She'd slept fitfully, worrying about Vinny's state of mind. He'd still been asleep when she'd left the house, but she'd propped a note up on the kitchen table between the salt and pepper shakers, telling him she loved him and to keep his chin up. Now she wondered whether that last bit had been a wise thing to write. How could he keep his bloody chin up when he felt guilty about not saving that old woman?

Leading the way into the station, Mike behind her, she headed for the front desk. "Anything come in?" she asked the night desk sergeant, Ursula Fringwell.

"No, all quiet for once." Ursula smiled. "Only one person brought in as well — aggravated assault."

"An easy shift for you then."

Ursula nodded. "Thankfully. I had a banging headache. I reckon it's this heat."

"Well, good luck getting to sleep in a hot bedroom today, love. It's already boiling out there. See you when we see you."

Bethany waved and legged it upstairs. Fran and Leona were already there, the eager buggers.

In her office, she sorted the paperwork and emails, then returned to the incident room to make everyone a coffee. It was past eight now, but before she had a meeting with her team, she needed to go and see Kribbs to let him know what was going on.

She took her coffee and another cup to his door then kick-tapped it by way of knocking.

"Come in," he said with a sigh.

That was unlike him. He was usually chipper no matter the time of day. Maybe she'd been right yesterday when she'd said he might have something on his mind.

She used her elbow to push down the door handle and went inside, placing his cup on the desk.

"Thanks, Beth. What can I do for you?"

"I'm just here to update you, sir. As you know, we had to leave your office yesterday in a bit of a rush. Murder. A Jason Holt." She sat on the chair opposite him. "I have to say, the victim was left in an unholy state."

Kribbs sipped his coffee. Swallowed loudly. "Tell me."

"He'd had a hole carved out of his midsection and all his innards removed."

Kribbs spluttered on his second sip. "Good grief."

"That's not all. His face had been taken off. The skin, I mean. He had red eyes — we're assuming contacts — and a white skull, also with red eyes, had been printed on some material and stuck to his chest."

"That is extremely disturbing."

"Hmm. No idea what that all means yet. We spoke to his employees. Found out he'd been seeing someone other than his wife."

"Could a love triangle bring *those* kinds of results, though? If so, that's one hell of an annoyed person. Could be his mistress — or maybe her other half if she has one. Or Holt's wife?"

"No, she was at work. Her alibi was checked out — solid. Seems he was seeing a young girl, possibly underage."

"Ah, a disgruntled father, perhaps."

"No idea." She drank some coffee. While it wasn't everyone's first choice, she did love a bit of Maxwell House. "His wife said he had a temper and could fly off the handle at times, and his friend from work, a supervisor, said similar, but he mentioned Mr Holt had simmered down since he'd got married."

"Seems to me he pissed off the wrong person for whatever reason."

"Too right."

"Do we know who this girl is?"

"No, unfortunately, and it's a delicate matter to bring up with the wife, but I might have to. Actually, his brother was coming up yesterday with their mother. I could put feelers out with him."

"While it isn't an ideal thing to have to tell a spouse, if doing so leads to catching the killer . . ."

"I know." She sighed. Sometimes, her job was difficult. "Well, that's where we are right now. I'll give Presley a ring later for the actual cause of death. Isabelle mentioned he'd fallen on a spike sticking up out of a hearth decoration."

"Isabelle Abbott, SOCO?"

"Yes."

"She's the one you need to get together with once all the photos have been loaded up so you can talk through the crime scene."

Was he trying to teach Grandmother to suck eggs or what? She'd been doing this job for years. Of *course* she'd know speaking with Isabelle could help her catch whoever had done this. She preferred to work just with Mike, though, and study the images together. Instead of saying that, she smiled and stood, giving him a bright smile and not an evil look. "I'll be getting on then."

She took her cup and left the room, disgruntled, and strode to her office in a huff. She'd give Isabelle a call right now, then Kribbs couldn't berate her for leaving the woman out of the equation as much as she usually did.

At her desk, she flopped in the chair and dialled.

"Isabelle Abbott speaking."

"Hi, it's Beth. Did you find those keys to Jason's office?"

"Yes. Some officers went over there last night. Nothing. I emailed you about it."

"Oh, I didn't see it. Might have gone into spam. Kribbs is asking about the scene photos. Anything for me I can pass on to him?"

"We have toe-partial footprints in the blood around the living room rug, but no clear size to go by. There are so many, they overlap. But it does look like a boot of some description, possibly a Timberland. The tread is a match going by eye, but we need to check that more thoroughly."

"Right, so a workman's boots? I know people have those for general wear, but seeing as Jason ran a building company . . ."

"I thought the same thing, although we've been bitten on the arse by assuming before, so by all means we should investigate that but also look at other aspects."

There was Grandmother and her basket of fucking eggs again.

"Indeed," Bethany said. "Still, it's given me some hope. I'll let you get on."

"Good luck!"

Bethany docked the phone and sat there for a moment to digest the news. A boot. Could it be one of the builders they'd spoken to yesterday? She hadn't had any vibes off them where she thought they could be involved. Unless one of them had been lying . . . She slapped her hand on the desk and forced herself to her feet.

In the incident room, she stood in front of the whiteboards and stared at what Leona had already written. A picture of Jason was stuck in the middle of one, and she realised with a jolt this was the first time she'd seen him with skin on his face. He'd been a good-looking bloke, resembling Ronan Keating, except Jason had a wider jaw and appeared more rugged.

"Where did this photo come from?" she asked, turning to face the others.

Mike glanced up, shrugged, then continued reading whatever was on his monitor. "Not from me. I'm checking out the builders' alibis."

"Oh, Facebook," Fran said. "That was the latest one he uploaded. Last week."

"So that's as close to now as we're going to get. A recent likeness. Good." Bethany scratched the end of her nose. "Nothing jumped out at you on social media yesterday then?"

"No." Fran shook her head. "I was only able to access it as a potential friend."

"Bugger, I forgot to let you know his passwords." She turned to Mike.

He got up, pulling his notebook out of his pocket, and walked over to Fran. She wrote the information down.

"I'll get on this now," she said.

"Leona, how did things go with looking into family and friends?" Bethany asked.

"His father is deceased. His mother and brother live in Cornwall. Nothing dodgy there. Mother and father have no siblings, so no aunts, uncles, or cousins, and all the grandparents have passed away."

"So he's literally just got his mum and brother. Right." Bethany was grateful. It was less people to dig into. "Friends?"

"Going by who comments the most on Jason's posts, a Sam King seems to be close to him."

"We spoke to him yesterday. Anyone else?"

"I wrote the names on the board."

Bethany hadn't had a chance to read it all, so she turned to look. All were names of his employees, so no other mates? Interesting.

Bethany faced them again. "Okay, here's something we found out yesterday. Jason had been seeing a young girl

— one who looked eighteen but might not have been. His wife is apparently unaware, according to Mr King, but that means nothing. Women's intuition and all that. She might well know but chose to keep it to herself. I need to tiptoe around her on that one, so we'll be visiting her at The Ringer Hotel, which is where she's staying while her home is a crime scene. Me and Mike will do that in a few — we'll speak to Jason's mother and brother, too. Also, Isabelle thinks the shoe treads in the blood are Timberland boots. So, we could be looking at them as builder's boots or just a coincidence that someone else was wearing them."

"Or they could have been worn on purpose, to send us towards the builders," Leona said.

Bethany's phone rang. She pulled it out of her pocket and answered. Isabelle.

"Hi," Bethany said.

"Hello again. I forgot to say when we did the walk-through, no weapon left at the scene, but a knife is missing from the block on the kitchen side. I'll email you a picture of what the others are like so you know what you're keeping an eye out for."

"Okay, thanks." Bethany shoved her phone away and repeated what Isabelle had said. "So the perpetrator may have gone there without a weapon. Does that mean they hadn't intended killing Jason, things got out of hand, and they grabbed the knife?"

"Or maybe they were going to kill them a different way but the situation changed," Fran suggested. "Going by his Facebook photos, he was a gym-goer, so he had some beef on him to be able to ward off an attacker. There are pictures of him with a row of treadmills behind him."

Bethany recalled Jason's shoulders at the scene. Muscly. "Okay, so poke into that angle. Did he annoy someone at the gym? Also, he had an eagle tattoo. See if that's a logo for some kind of gang. All right, he's older now, but he might have belonged to one as a youngster and it's followed him into adulthood. Was he brought up in Shadwell?"

"I dealt with that yesterday, following his footpath, and yes, he was born here," Leona said. "His parents and brother moved down to Cornwall five years ago, then his father died. Heart attack at work."

Bethany glanced at the board — all the information was there. "Sorry, I shouldn't be asking when it's already written down. Okay, it's nearing nine now so, Mike, we'll get off to The Ringer to talk to the Holts. Oh, hang on." She checked her emails on her phone. One from Isabelle. "I'll forward you this picture of the missing knife. Catch you later, guys."

She sent the image then left the room, going down to the front desk. Rob stood behind it, typing away on his keyboard. He looked up and smiled.

"Morning, Rob. Anything?"

"Nope. Lucky you."

She laughed. "We'll be at The Ringer with the Holts in case you need us."

"Okie dokie." He diverted his attention to his monitor.

In the car, Bethany waited for Mike to buckle up, then she pulled away.

"None of JJ Builder's employees had Timberlands on," Mike said. "Saves you stressing about it."

"I didn't even think to see what they were all wearing, though I must confess, Sam King with his bare chest caught my eye."

"Hey, you. Married woman."

"Not in *that* way, Christ." She turned right. "Just in the I-didn't-know-where-to-look way. It was uncomfortable."

"Is that how you feel when you're on holiday and everyone's parading about half naked?"

"Um, no. That's different. To sit at a table with a shirtless stranger is a bit disconcerting. Well, it was for me anyway. Clearly, you didn't have a problem with it."

"I didn't take much notice. I was too steamed up about that other fella saying Jason might have been seeing a minor."

"Hmm, we really need to find out who she is." She paused. "Come to think of it, I *did* notice what Sam was wearing. Skinny jeans and boots, although I can't be sure if they were Timberlands."

She pulled up in the gravelled front car park at The Ringer, one of the top-end hotels in the city. It must have been a stately home or something similar in its heyday, the windows made up of several small squares, each of them glinting in the sunlight, reflecting the clear blue sky. The dark brick and black beams gave it an imposing air. A fountain spurted water in the centre of a rectangle of grass bordered by flowers in yellows and reds. Ivy had crept halfway up the right-hand side, its next journey to curl around the top windows.

They got out, and Bethany clicked her key fob to lock the vehicle. A set of white double doors were open, so they walked through into a flagstone-floored reception with what appeared to be an old bar as a desk. The murky interior was so dark a lamp beamed out light on a tall table.

Bethany approached the desk and pressed the old-fashioned brass bell.

A woman appeared from a room to the right, where a few people sat with cups of tea and newspapers. Black pencil skirt, white blouse, her auburn hair in the tightest chignon Bethany had ever seen. She tottered behind the desk on silver high heels.

"Good morning. Welcome to The Ringer. How may I help you?"

Bethany showed her ID. "We're here to see the Holt family, specifically Georgia."

"Ah, yes, they did mention at breakfast you might be arriving." The woman, about forty, smiled. "Although Georgia did say she wasn't sure if you'd definitely be here. She's in room fifteen, first floor." She pointed to a lift on the left. "Elizabeth and Warren have the rooms either side — Elizabeth is in fourteen, Warren sixteen."

Warren must be the brother.

"Okay, thank you."

Bethany and Mike moved to the lift, and he pressed the call button. The door slid open, and they stepped on,

Mike again prodding the button. Enclosed, the car moving upwards, Bethany shivered. She hated confined spaces.

"Someone walk over your grave?" Mike asked.

"No. You know I can't stand these things. Especially when I know what happens if you're stuck in one during a fire, Vinny said—"

"Don't . . ." Mike warned. "How is Vinny anyway?"

"Upset. Bad job yesterday."

"Do I need to get him out for a drink?"

"Would you?"

"Yep. I could do with a chinwag myself."

"Thanks. I never know what to say to him when depression hits."

The lift slid to a smooth stop, and the doors eased apart. They walked into the hallway, and room fifteen was to the right. Bethany knocked on sixteen instead and waited.

"Let's see if Jason's brother is willing to spill secrets, shall we?" she muttered.

CHAPTER EIGHT

Warren Holt was the spitting image of his brother. So much so, it gave Bethany a jolt when he flung back the door. It must be painful for his mother to see him. Or perhaps it was a comfort.

She held up her ID, as did Mike.

"Oh, hello." Warren frowned.

"Can we come in for a moment? We need to ask you a couple of questions," she said, sliding her ID away.

"I didn't have anything to do with this." He stared at her with red-rimmed eyes, hands up, palms facing her. They shook, as though he honestly believed he was in trouble.

"I didn't say you did." She smiled in the hopes he'd feel more at ease. "I just said we needed to ask questions. Nothing to worry about, I assure you."

"Right. Yes." He stepped back in a narrow hallway just about wide enough for one person.

Bethany and Mike went inside, and she wondered whether Warren sounded like Jason, too. If that were the case, how did Liz Holt cope with *that*?

She quickly took in the area. On the right, a bathroom boasted a white free-standing tub on stout, gold-coloured feet, a shower cubicle, and an inset sink with a black marble surround shot through with white lightning strikes. Ahead, at the end of the hallway was a spacious bedroom-cum-living room, the bed dressed in white. A black leather sofa and chair stood to the right, and a mahogany coffee table squatted on a burgundy paisley rug with ivory tassels in perfect lines.

Warren sat in the chair, which squeaked beneath his weight, Mike on one end of the sofa and Bethany on the other, closest to Warren. Mike got his notebook out and cleared his throat.

"I just need a bit of background first," she said, "then I have a delicate question I need to ask, okay?"

"Delicate?" He frowned.

"Yes, we'll get to that in a minute. Where were you last night?"

"What, you think *I* did this?" The skin beside his eyes twitched.

"Please answer the question."

"I was in the pub, alone, but the manager chatted to me for a bit."

"What's the pub called, and where is it?"

"The Blue Anchor Inn, Coinagehall Street, Helston."

Mike got his phone out, probably texting Fran or Leona to check that alibi.

"How did you get on with Jason?" She watched his face.

His forehead lines smoothed out, and his mouth lifted upwards at the corners, creating laughter lines. A genuine reaction. "He was my best friend. We stuck by each other all through our childhood, only veering off to make friends with others once we got to secondary school. Twins tend to be separated in classes then."

So that was why they looked so alike. "Identical?"

"We are. I'm older by a minute."

She wondered if that had been something he'd felt he had to mention his whole life, just so there was a difference between them. "What would you say wasn't the same about you?"

"He was a bit hard-nosed at times. I don't get annoyed unless I'm backed into a corner. I prefer to talk things through instead of punching, although he packed that in once he met Georgia. She's so kind-hearted, she can't bear fighting. He stopped getting into scraps to please her."

"So he loved her then."

"God, yes."

"What about tattoos? Do you have any?"

"We both got eagles on our wrists when we were eighteen."

"Can I have a look? I didn't get a chance to see Jason's."

He pulled up his sleeve and presented his arm. An elegant eagle spanned his wrist, as though in flight.

"Thank you. Do you use social media?"

"No. Can't stand it." He adjusted his sleeve.

That would explain why Warren didn't come up on Jason's feed or comments.

"Did Jason have many friends?" Maybe there were others who also didn't use Facebook or Twitter, people he classed as mates.

"Not really. As I said, we had each other for years, and I think it was the same for the pair of us, that one extra friend was enough, you know? His was Sam — Sam King. Other than that, his employees. They were more like a bunch of buddies than anything. He never mentioned anyone else."

"Were you close enough for him to confide secrets?" she asked. With them being twins, she guessed they were.

"Um, not sure what you're classing as a secret." He raised his eyebrows.

"Okay, let's try this another way, a direct way. Did Jason tell you any secrets?"

Warren nodded. "Plenty over the years."

"I want to focus on, say, the past few months. Did he spill any recently? If so, would any of them mean someone would want to kill him?"

"I doubt it." He half laughed.

It annoyed her a little. This wasn't a laughing matter. Perhaps he was nervous. "How about you tell me the secrets so we can go from there? I can then decide if they're along the lines of what we've been told."

Warren shifted, clearly uncomfortable with the direction things were going in. "All right. I suppose it'll be okay. It's not like he's here to get in trouble for it anymore, is it." He took a deep breath then let it out slowly. "He stole a chainsaw once out of a client's garage in the early days when he was just setting up. He needed one, couldn't afford it, so nicked it. Felt bloody guilty and all, so when he started making money, he bought a new one and had it sent to the bloke he'd nabbed it off."

So he had a conscience.

"I doubt someone would kill him over a saw," she said. "How about a bigger secret."

"It's just stuff like that, nothing really major, and it doesn't even seem important now he's dead, if you see what I mean. What's pinching a bloody saw compared to being killed?"

He had a point there.

"Anything he was doing that he shouldn't be, specifically while married?"

He shook his head. "I'm not sure what you mean." His eyebrows drew down.

Time to be blunt, spell it out. "An affair."

"Jason? No! He adored Georgia."

Not enough to keep his dick in his pants. "I see. Unfortunately, it's come to light that he was seeing someone else."

"I don't believe it." He stared, his expression one of a gobsmacked man, his eyebrows now high and arched.

"We don't have proof, nor do we know who she is, but two people have mentioned it. She's young — possibly too young."

Warren barked out a harsh laugh, sounding more like *ha!* "Absolutely no way would he go with someone who was underage."

"She looks older so may have lied. He might not have known."

"Even so, why would a man closer to forty than he liked to admit opt to go with someone so young?"

"Closer than he liked to admit?"

"He was a bit naffed at nearing what he'd always considered 'older territory'."

Mike coughed. Bethany hid a smile.

"Which might have led to a mid-life crisis?" she suggested.

"No. That's nuts. I just can't imagine him even looking at another woman, let alone going with one. Sorry, I don't buy it." Warren stood and paced, pinching his chin. "I mean, he would have told me, surely."

"What is your stance on affairs?"

"I think it's disgusting."

"Hence why he didn't tell you, maybe?"

He stopped his back and forth and sat, elbows on his knees, and rested his forehead in his hands. "I can't get over this. What the hell was he playing at? Georgia's a lovely woman, one of the kindest I know. She doesn't deserve this." He paused. "Does she know?"

"We have no idea. Sam King kept it from his wife in case she told Georgia, so I suspect she's unaware. The other man who mentioned it said he'd remained closed-lipped about it because he didn't want to upset Georgia. All the employees have a healthy respect for her."

"So they should. Will you tell her?"

"I'm going to have to ask her about it, I'm afraid."

"It'll crush her."

"I realise that, but we have a killer to catch, and keeping this sort of information from her may be detrimental to the case. Despite it upsetting her, we have a duty to follow all leads and must question her."

"I understand. Do me a favour and speak to her alone, will you? I can't imagine she'll want me or Mum seeing her humiliation."

"Of course. We'll go and see your mother now, then Georgia. Please refrain from speaking to your mum — no giving her a quick text message — until we've left the hotel. Jason may well have confided in her, and I'd like to see a genuine reaction."

"Certainly."

Bethany rose, and Mike followed suit.

"Thank you for your time," she said. "And I'm sorry for your loss."

"I'll never get over it. Half of me is gone."

She turned away at that, unable to stand seeing the pain in his eyes, and a lump engulfed her throat to the point it hurt. What must it be like to lose the other half of yourself?

She left the room, and once Mike stood beside her in the corridor and the door had closed, she leant against the wall and shut her eyes to take a moment to compose herself. She wanted to cry — really cry — but professionalism won out, and she snapped her eyes open, told herself off, and knocked on Liz Holt's door.

It opened, and a woman in her sixties stood there, her shoulder-length blonde hair threaded with thick strands of grey, her eyes red and sore-looking. The end of her nose appeared to have been wiped numerous times. Her puffy cheeks and inflated bags beneath her eyes spoke of a broken mother, her son lost to her in a senseless killing that would haunt her until her dying day.

ID on display, Bethany smiled. "We need to come in for a moment."

Liz led them into an identical room to Warren's, and they sat in the same places as they had in his. Bethany asked similar questions, and when it came to the one about the affair, Liz howled, tears streaking her face.

"I hated knowing," she said on a sob. "Hated it, but he was my son, and I promised I'd stay quiet. He needed someone to talk to. The woman wouldn't back off."

"Do you know how he met her? Georgia said they rarely socialised."

"Yes, she was hanging around the yard — the business. She kept walking past the entrance, looking lost, and Jason went out there to see if she was okay. They got talking, and she said she lived with a violent father. Then she cried, and he offered to take her into the bungalow so she could sort herself out, maybe have a cup of tea."

"I see. What happened then?"

"He didn't have sex with her that day. I think he said it was after a few weeks of her visiting, always on a Wednesday, and they'd grown close with her confiding in him, and one thing led to another. He was distraught straight after, felt guilty right away, and once she'd gone, he phoned me and confessed the lot. Then a week or so later he told me it had happened again — a few times. Said he hadn't been able to stop himself. Of course, I was devastated. Georgia is like a daughter to me, so I was torn on what to do."

"Does she know?"

"Good heavens, she's never mentioned it to me, and what would I have said to her if she'd ever said anything? I couldn't betray my son. You understand?"

Bethany didn't have children, but yes, she imagined she'd be the same. Her duty would be to her flesh and blood, regardless of whether she was fond of Georgia.

"I'm going to have to ask her, you realise that, don't you?" she said.

Liz nodded and wiped her eyes with a soggy tissue. "Yes, but is it possible for me to be kept out of this? I don't want her to know I was aware all along."

"We'll try, but I can't promise anything. Our priority is finding Jason's killer."

"Yes, yes, of course."

"Do you know the woman's name?"

"Chelsea, but as for her surname, no."

"Were you aware she might be underage?"

"What?" she choked out. "Surely not."

"Someone mentioned they thought she might be."

"Dear God . . . What was he thinking?"

Bethany grimaced. The thing was, Jason clearly *hadn't* been thinking.

CHAPTER NINE

Georgia looked a wreck. Bethany studied her from the sofa in her room, feeling sorry for her and wishing she could turn back time and make everything go away. This case had affected Bethany more than any other. The thought of losing Vinny like this . . . she couldn't even begin to imagine.

She couldn't change anything, though, so instead she'd try to make this as painless as possible so the woman could take the first step on the path to moving on without the love of her life. It would be hard, but what else was there to do except love his memory and learn to smile and laugh again, perhaps as he'd have wanted her to?

"How are you?" she asked her, then felt bad, because she was clearly heartbroken. *What an insensitive thing to say, you silly mare.*

Georgia had obviously had a heavy dose of reality hitting her since yesterday. Passing the nighttime hours alone with her thoughts had opened her eyes to what had happened — she was a widow, her stability gone, her emotions cast adrift on an ocean of despair. How utterly awful. She'd undoubtedly been left all the money and property, but what was that compared to living the rest of your life without your husband? Your soul mate?

Money meant nothing in the face of such loss.

"I'm . . . I'm bearing up. Just." She managed a meek smile, her eyes damp with the threat of fresh tears.

Bethany cringed inside. This woman was 'bearing up', and here was Bethany, about to make everything a whole lot worse. The man Georgia thought she'd married was someone else entirely. A cheater and, despite the fact he'd felt guilty afterwards, he hadn't felt guilty enough at the time to resist another few trysts, letting desire sweep him away, until the depth of what he'd done by breaking his marriage vows had sent him to the one person he knew would forgive him — his mother.

"Okay, have you remembered anything that might help us?"

"No, but I noticed something in my bedroom when I was packing a bag yesterday before I came here, and I told Miss Abbott."

Bethany wondered why Isabelle hadn't passed it on. "What was that?"

"Some of my jewellery is missing, and my Swarovski crystals — a swan and a teardrop. They're only small, not worth an awful amount, maybe four hundred secondhand, but they have sentimental value. Jason bought them for me."

Georgia's version of them not being worth much was vastly different to Bethany's. Four hundred was a heck of a lot of money. She kept the shock off her face — she hoped.

"And the jewellery?"

"A pair of diamond earrings and a matching necklace. They'd fetch quite a bit. Maybe five thousand."

"Did Jason buy those, too?"

"Yes. Once his business took off, he was earning insane amounts. I can't afford that sort of thing on my wages."

"Do you have pictures of them?"

"The earrings and necklace, yes, but not the crystals, but you could see similar online. I'll just find them for you."

Georgia seemed to have perked up somewhat. Perhaps doing something constructive like this helped to keep the grief at bay. Bethany imagined if it was her, she'd have to throw herself into her job more than she usually did in order to get through something like this. She couldn't bear to think about it.

Georgia turned her phone around and showed the crystals. Then she switched to her photo album and brought up an image of her wearing the jewellery.

"Can you email those to me, please?" Bethany asked.

"Yes."

Bethany recited her email address. She'd send the pictures to Leona and Fran so they could alert the local pawn shop owners that if anyone came in trying to get rid of them, they should phone the police as soon as possible — and ensure their CCTV was working, possibly keeping the seller talking until uniforms arrived. A big ask for a civilian, especially when the person in question had carved a hole in a body and skinned his face.

Was it wise to expect them to do that?

No. Best that they just press their panic button if they have one and act normally.

Her phone pinged with an email alert, and she quickly forwarded it to the girls in the incident room along with an explanation message, knowing she was holding off the inevitable. She had to get on with the questioning, though.

She took a deep breath and plunged in. "I'm sorry to have to ask this, but we need to cover all possibilities and scenarios. Do you think Jason would have ever cheated on you?"

"Oh." Georgia stared down and fiddled with her fingers. She'd been biting the skin beside her nails by the looks of it. "I wondered when that would come up."

"You know?" *Well, that makes things much easier.*

Georgia raised her head and nodded, her cheeks red. "He didn't know I knew, though."

"How did you find out?"

Georgia sighed for England, France, the whole world. "I . . . I went into his office unannounced once. The one at the yard."

"Oh dear." Bethany's heart sank. *What a bloody appalling way to find out.*

"He hadn't locked the door," Georgia went on. "I don't know if you noticed, but it has a handle, and you can lock it by turning it upwards. He must have forgotten to do that."

"Go on."

"Well, I dropped in before one of my morning shifts. There was a query on Twitter he needed to see — someone wanted an extension built on the back of their house. It was a big job and worth a lot of money, something he'd want to know about right away. He never bothered with the business side of social media, that was my department. Anyway, he wasn't in the office, so I checked the other rooms. I thought he'd gone for a nap in the bedroom — he'd been tossing and turning the night before — and when I looked through the open doorway . . ." She bit her lip.

"Oh, Georgia, I'm *so* sorry." She was, too. The devastation of that must have been immense. How did you move on from that? With trust crumbled, what was left?

Georgia gave a watery smile. "I left quietly, never said a word. They were so . . . busy, I doubt they even heard the front door close."

"Did you get a look at her?" It was possibly cruel to have asked that, but with no leads, she had to push for something.

"Not her face, no. She was . . . um . . . sitting on him." He breath hitched, and her chin quivered. "With her back to me. But she was slim — petite. And she had long blonde hair. The ends nearly reached her bum. Funny what you remember, isn't it?"

What a truly terrible thing to have walked in on.

"There's talk that she's young," Bethany said gently.

"That doesn't surprise me."

Oh. Bethany hadn't expected that. What else hadn't Georgia told them? "What do you mean?"

"Some men have a wandering eye, even when you're with them. They can't help themselves. They think you don't notice." She huffed out a sad laugh. "He always stared at young blondes. I was hurt by it, thought it was rude of him — even to do it when I wasn't there — and it made me jealous — but, and this will sound so sad, I loved him anyway."

Had Georgia put up with it for love or money? A wicked thing to contemplate, but Bethany had to remain objective.

"Why didn't you tell him what you'd seen?" she asked, curious.

"His temper."

"I see. Did you fear he'd hurt you?"

"No, I just didn't want him going into one of his rages, and he'd have sulked for days, making me feel as though it was my fault, and I considered that, you know. Wondered what I'd done wrong if he was looking at other women — *doing it* with them. What wasn't I giving him? That sort of thing tends to go round and round. So many thoughts go through your head. You hope they'll go away, but they don't."

Could Georgia have organised the hit? Gone to work for a cast-iron alibi while someone else did the dirty work?

He was a bastard, in Bethany's opinion, but he didn't deserve what had happened to him. "Did you ever think of leaving him?"

"I did, but then he changed, went back to normal. I assume the time he'd been on edge and snappy was when he was seeing her. Guilty conscience? Was he thinking of leaving me and didn't know how to say it? That was a big question for me, and I had to work out what I'd do if he told me it was over for us. Then shortly after I caught them, he was his usual self, so I guessed they'd finished."

"Would you have continued in your marriage if you found out he'd done it again, either with her or someone else?" *She has a name. Chelsea. But I can't for the life of me tell you that. A name makes it more real.*

"No. Once, I can forgive, but not twice."

"We really need to find out who she is. Unfortunately, no one seems to know." *I need a surname, then we're cooking with gas.*

"Did you ask Warren and Liz?" Georgia asked, head cocked to one side.

Was she fishing? Watching Bethany's face for a reaction? Was she checking to see if one of them knew and hadn't told her?

"Yes. They have no idea." Bethany wasn't lying. Neither of them knew the girl's surname, and her answer was a diversion so she wouldn't have to admit Liz knew about the affair. If she was like a mother to Georgia, they needed each other to pull through, and being at loggerheads over this wouldn't help matters. "Okay, we need to get on now. If you remember anything else, please give me or the FLO, Alice, a call."

"Thank you."

Bethany and Mike left, and in the lift, she held her breath until they reached the lobby. Emotions warred inside her — compassion, sorrow, anger towards Jason — and she struggled to keep them from wrenching her insides. She waved to the receptionist on their way out, and once they were in the car, she let a few tears fall to ease the tumult raging through her.

"You all right, Beth?" Mike placed a hand on her shoulder and squeezed.

His touch was almost her undoing. "That was a bit emotional."

"I must admit, I had a lump in my throat at one point," he said. "That poor woman. Although, harsh as it sounds, we must bear in mind she could be behind this."

"I know, and I so don't want her to be. She needs a happy ending." Time for a change of subject. "Fancy a quick coffee? Fran, Leona, or Isabelle haven't rung, so there's nothing we need to rush back for. Plus, I kind of need five minutes, know what I mean?"

"Yep, okay."

She headed for Costa and parked in a spare bay out the front. Inside, Mike grabbed a seat by the window, and Bethany paid for cappuccinos, the froth thick on top with a flower on it created from cinnamon. She sat opposite him, and they sipped in silence, Bethany looking around at the nearly full tables. Mothers with squawking preschool kids. Mothers with well-behaved kids. Businessmen and women eating cakes, cookies, or Danish, trying not to get crumbs on their expensive suits. All of them with thoughts, maybe worrying about getting a parking ticket or being late paying the electric bill. Then there was Mike and herself, sitting with their heads bursting with images of blood, a body with its insides scooped out, red eyes, a skull image, a family torn asunder, an affair, and a killer who had taken their time — someone who knew Jason would be alone all night. Or they didn't care if Georgia came back and caught them.

Had that happened, would they have killed her, too?

How she wished she was that woman over there right now, who was taking a selfie, more concerned with whether her nonexistent double chin showed if she didn't hold the phone up at the correct angle.

Insignificant worries. Some would say ridiculous in the grand scheme of things. But those worries were big to those people. They shaped their days, their lives, directed their next moves. Kept them awake at night.

If they had in their heads what Bethany had in hers, how would they react?

Better that they worried about Danish flakes sticking to their clothes.

Her phone rang, drawing her out of her head and into the present. Rob Quarry's name sat there on her screen, and she dreaded what he was about to say.

"Yep." She held her breath.

"Sorry, but there's been a call about a woman called Opal Forrester. She didn't show up for work, so her boss rang Miss Forrester's mother, who was highly concerned, given the fact Miss Forrester has been in the news lately."

"What for?" And why was this anything to do with Bethany and Mike?

"An abortion gone wrong. Well, that's what the public have been led to believe. Don't you read the news?"

"Not if I can bloody help it, no."

"Well, what actually happened was the young girl had a previously undiagnosed heart condition. Long story short, she used fake ID at a private clinic to get an abortion. They didn't check — and to be honest, do they? Not sure — and she died on the table. Miss Forrester has been hounded by the press ever since. She phoned her mother last night, sounding worried, asking if she was okay, and now . . ."

"Don't tell me she's dead."

"She is. And she's in the same state as Jason Holt."

"Fuck it!" The words burst out of her mouth before she had a chance to stop them.

People turned her way and stared, and she held up her free hand and mouthed *sorry*.

"Okay, address?" she asked.

Rob gave it to her.

"I take it SOCO are already there?" *Of course they will be, you daft cow.*

"Yes, been there for a while."

"Right, we'll go now." She put her phone away.

Mike raised his eyebrows. "Another one?"

"Yes. I'll explain on the way. Fuck me sideways. This is turning into a bloody nightmare."

They left Costa and slung themselves into the car.

On the way, she told Mike what Rob had said.

"So Miss Forrester has got to be connected to Jason," Mike said, running a hand through his hair. It stuck up, and he patted it back down while nosing in the mirror on the sun visor.

"Well, it's too much of a coincidence to be unrelated. Two different people just don't go around taking insides out of bodies, do they. And, God, this is way out of our league. We haven't dealt with anything as gross as this before, and what if it turns into a serial? It only takes one more."

"Then we deal with it." He pressed the window button to let in some air.

"You know it might be passed over to serious crimes. I don't want them to have it. This is our case. What if Kribbs insists I get hold of that Tracy Collier woman? I mean, have you heard about how many serials she's had to deal with?

She's a pro. If I need advice, I'll get hold of her, but she's not taking over."

"She moved to the next town, didn't she?"

"Yes. Shit, what if she *has* to take this one? What if we have no choice in the matter?" Much as this was a case rapidly getting out of control, Bethany was desperate to do it herself, with Mike, not with a woman she'd heard was hard as nails with a nasty mouth on her.

"You're worrying before you need to, and to be fair, you sound a bit hysterical. Word is she won't come back to the city if she can help it, so I doubt she'll get involved," Mike said. "Something to do with her father — the Collier case."

"Oh yes, that was the talk of the station. Okay. Deep breath. If I do end up speaking to her, hopefully she'll tell us to go and fuck ourselves, which is her preferred way of talking apparently. I didn't have much to do with her when she worked here. We were DCs back then. Christ, where has the time gone?"

"It's certainly flown. Look, we can manage very well on our own, that's what I think. We've been dealing with murder for years. All right, we've never done a serial — and anyway, Tracy dealt with that sort of thing when she was here — but still, how hard can it be? It's still just a case."

"I have a feeling we're going to find out how hard. Anyway, we're here, and unless Kribbs suggests it gets moved to Tracy, I'm keeping my mouth shut."

CHAPTER TEN

They left the car and walked up the path. Tory stood on the doorstep with the log, something she always opted to do. She wasn't one for door-to-door. Said she didn't have the patience for questioning people.

They signed it, togged up from head to toe, and walked inside.

SOCO floated about doing their thing on the lower level, and with evidence markers dotted around on the floors and surfaces, she assumed all the photos had been taken, although, scrub that, a camera clicked somewhere off in the distance, probably upstairs. The place was clean and tidy, minimalist, as though no one lived there at all. No knick-knacks, photos, or personal effects.

Isabelle came down the stairs and met them in the living room doorway. "Ah, you're here. The quick version is, the killer doesn't seem to have been in any of these rooms on this floor, although we've marked things that could be relevant: fluff on the laminate, smear marks in the kitchen on the worktop — could be butter on a finger but may yield foreign prints. Hair, although it's the same colour as the victim's, but you never know. Stuff like that. Upstairs, however . . ."

"Rob said it was a similar deal as with Jason."

"Yes, Opal Forrester was treated much the same way, except she didn't bang her head on a hearth point. Someone seems to have whacked her with a hammer instead."

"Why the hammer?" Bethany asked. "Why deviate?"

"Who knows?" Isabelle shrugged. "Maybe Jason being almost certainly knocked out by hitting his head gave the killer ideas — you know, the victim is unconscious or dead, making it easier to remove their innards and skin them."

"I've been thinking about that. It takes time to do what they've done, so I have a strong feeling they know the victims or at least have been keeping tabs on them, their movements, and have knowledge on whether anyone will come along and disturb them."

"Then it's a case of seeing if the victims have a connection. Are you coming up for a look?" Isabelle asked.

"I just need to send Fran a message quickly, tell her there's another murder, get her and Leona looking for a connection."

She did that, then followed Isabelle and Mike up the cream-carpeted stairs. No markers, no blood, completely clean to the naked eye, but forensics would find anything seemingly invisible.

"The bathroom has a similar deal to Jason's," Isabelle said, showing them inside the small space. "Blood, although incredibly faint, left in the bath around the plughole, except this time they were careful not to leave smears elsewhere, like on the door or sink. There was a strong smell of bleach in here when we arrived, and tests will confirm whether the room has been cleaned recently. The other rooms, apart from Opal's, are clear and don't appear to have been disturbed. Prints and whatnot have been done regardless. So, on to the main bedroom . . ."

Bethany sucked in a breath, readying herself to see another eviscerated body.

And there she was, Opal Forrester, laid out on the blood-soaked bed, the skin of her face gone, her hair matted in clumps on the pillow, and the side of her head . . . Oh

God, the side of her head was staved in, an obvious hole made by the circular end of a hammer.

"Jesus Christ . . ." Mike said beside Bethany, the words ragged. "That poor woman."

Bethany swallowed down bile. The hole in Opal's stomach had been gouged out in a cleaner manner somehow, as though the killer had done a test run on Jason and had thought about how he could do it better this time — more scraping, the inner cavity smoother.

"Her stomach," she said.

"Yes, and I know exactly how that was done." Isabelle pointed to a hoover like a Dyson in the corner.

Bethany stared at it. The transparent dirt collector was half full of red matter. "What the hell?"

"I know. Absolutely shocking." Isabelle shuddered.

"This is too much," Mike said. "A *hoover*? Who even *thinks* of doing that?"

"A sick bastard, obviously." Isabelle turned back to Opal. "Same skull image on the chest. We haven't touched her yet — waiting on Presley so he can see her position et cetera — but I'm assuming it's been glued on."

A thought hit Bethany then, so she sent a message to Fran: CHECK SALES OF RED CONTACT LENSES.

"I just can't work out what all this means," she said. "And ruddy hell, it's hot in here, or is it me?" Sweat beaded on her upper lip, and she used the cuff of her protective suit to wipe it away. "There are so many people we'll need to speak to on this one. Did you know she was in the news recently?" she asked Isabelle.

"Yes. Maybe a journalist is a good place to start after her mother." Isabelle peered over Bethany's shoulder, out onto the landing.

Bethany turned. Presley had arrived, and he came in, shaking his head.

"I was in the middle of Jason Holt's PM. I really don't like stopping halfway through." He stood beside the bed, snorted air through his nose, nostrils flaring, popped his bag on top of a steel evidence step, and took out his pad. While sketching, he said, "That cavity is a lot neater than Holt's."

"Used a hoover on it," Isabelle said, nonchalant, like this was *normal*.

"Dear Lord." Presley cleared his throat. "She's been tied at some point then."

Bethany studied the body. Although blood covered her, white stripes indeed showed her skin had been covered up with something on her wrists and ankles. There were scalloped edges. "Rope, going by that pattern."

"Yes. And, hmm, her pyjama top being sliced down the middle . . ." Presley pointed with his pen. "With the material bunched by her sides and soaked with blood, we can't see anything, and I bet it's all dry and hard by now, but I'll let you know once she's at the morgue whether there are stab marks on the material. Jason was completely shirtless. Why, when this young lady is still wearing hers . . . after a fashion?"

"Maybe he has more respect for women," Mike suggested.

Bethany almost laughed. "But he killed her! Hardly a respectful thing to do. Anyway, it doesn't matter. Clothed or not, it's the same sodding person doing this. I can't get over that hoover." She shook her head.

Presley finished drawing Opal's position and making notes. "I'll take her temperature in a sec."

"Anything from Jason's PM you can pass on yet?" Bethany asked.

"Cause of death was the whack to the head from the hearth spike. Penetrated the brain, blah, blah, blah. I see Opal here has a big gash, too. Seems our person likes holes in heads. Lovely."

"A hammer, I guessed," Isabelle said. "Seen enough of those sorts of marks in my last posting in Somerset to know what to look for."

"I was just going to say the same thing." Presley removed the thermometer from Opal's ear. "She died last night. About ten or eleven." He lifted her arm. "Like with Jason, rigor is almost gone. Christ, it stinks in here. That's a mix of summer heat and dried blood for you."

At the reminder of the smell, Bethany breathed through her mouth. The air was cloying, what with no window open and the sun beaming directly on the window. She took in the blood-splattered walls, the floor, the bedding. An absolute mess signifying the end of a life. No one imagined going out this way, or if they did, it didn't seem possible it could happen to them. It was always someone else, wasn't it? Had Opal known what was coming, or had she been smacked with that hammer while she'd slept?

I hope it's the latter.

"We're going to have to visit her mother," Bethany said, her guts churning. "Any weapons found?"

Isabelle twitched her nose. "All knives are in the block, but there are a few in a drawer in the kitchen. No telling whether any are missing. No hammer present. Different boot sole marks this time, though."

Bethany checked the floor. Carpet. A lot of spatter. "I don't see a footprint."

"On the bed." Isabelle raised her eyebrows, as though Bethany was slacking and should have already seen it.

She wouldn't bite. Yes, she should have seen it, but presented with so much visual horror, it was difficult sometimes to take it all in when your brain was reeling.

There they were, two or three partial prints on the sheet either side of Opal. So they'd stood on the bed. Why?

Bethany sighed. "Okay, we really need to go. If you get anything else significant . . ."

"Yep, I'll ring you." Isabelle smiled.

"I'll finish Jason's PM later and email you," Presley said. "I'll probably have to do this one tomorrow."

Bethany nodded, and with Mike behind her, left the house, her muscles bunched tight. They took their suits, gloves, and booties off on the doorstep and deposited them in a large plastic container. Once in the car, seat belts on, she looked across at Mike.

"A hoover, though," he said.

"I know." She shook her head, flabbergasted. Then she rang Rob. "Can you find me the address for Opal Forrester's mother, please? I'll hang on while you do it."

"Yep, give me a minute or two."

While she waited, she said to Mike, "Whoever this is . . . they're deranged. Like, seriously. Nice cage, no bird, know what I mean?"

"They're scary, actually. I don't think I'll sleep well tonight. Part of me wishes Collier *would* take it off our hands."

"You're joking. Please tell me you're fucking about."

"Um, I wasn't, but I suppose it's in my best interests to say I was, so you don't bite my head off." He grinned and knuckled his eyes. "D'you know, I just can't unsee images in my head of the killer vacuuming inside someone's body." He dropped his hands to his lap and tilted his head back, staring into space.

A surge of determination rose in Bethany. "I want to nail the bastard. You and me, Fran and Leona. Isabelle. Our team. No one else."

"Ready to get on with it then?"

"Yep," she said, and damn it, she was.

Rob's breathing on the line caught her attention. "Beth? Ready to take this down?"

"Yep."

"Forty-nine Juniper Berry Drive. A Nancy Forrester."

"Okay, thanks." She ended the call and drove off, turning left. "She only lives a couple of streets away, the poor cow."

"Fancy getting this sort of news on a lovely day like this," Mike said. "It feels like it should be raining, a storm. No one wants one of their deepest fears coming true, and we're just about to go and wreck someone's life. I sound like a cracked record, but this bit really is shit."

She swerved right into Juniper, narrowly avoiding some stupid teenager practising wheelies. Angry, she stopped and opened her window. "Do you like living?" she asked him.

The kid gawked at her, ginger eyelashes rising and falling rapidly.

"I suspect your mum wouldn't like you dicing with death, so go to the park and fuck around — *don't* do it on the road, okay?" She drove away and carried on as if she hadn't broken her convo with Mike. "I agree, but it's got to be done, so we may as well get it over with." She slowed so she could check the numbers.

Forty-nine's red front door looked recently painted, all fresh and glossy, and the silver door knocker glinted in the direct sunlight. Red and yellow flowers, a bit worse for wear, shrivelled from too much heat and not enough water, bent to one side, their petals crusty on the edges. One touch of a fingertip, and they'd crumble to dust. She parked beside a lamppost and waited for Mike to join her on the pavement. On the way up the cement path, she eyed the nets in the windows, wondering if they were meant to be cream or were just extremely dirty.

A blonde woman of about fifty-five opened the door before Bethany had a chance to knock. A cigarette dangled from her mouth, and she reared back from the smoke, mascara-thick lashes wafting up and down. Bethany guessed the nets were covered in eau de fag aroma, sending them discoloured.

She held up her ID. "DI Bethany Smith, and this is my partner, DS Mike Wilkins. We're here about Opal, and it's best we come in."

The ciggie dropped from her mouth, bounced on the doorstep, then rolled onto the grass. A tube of ash sat forlornly on the path. "No . . . Don't tell me this is serious. What's happened?" She stepped back and pressed herself onto the wall, one hand at her neck.

Bethany stamped the fag out, then she and Mike walked inside. Mike closed the door. The stench of old smoke hung heavy where it had seeped into the walls and carpets.

"Come on, Mrs Forrester, I'll make us all a cup of tea." Bethany guided her into a kitchen and made sure the woman sat at the table. Then she flung open the window. "You don't mind, do you? It's hot in here." Fresh air floated inside, and Bethany felt less like she'd walked into a fog of nicotine. She flicked the still-hot kettle on and got busy sorting mugs. "Can you tell me what time Opal rang you last night?"

Nancy clutched at her head, her cerise nail varnish visible through the pale strands. "Um . . . maybe about half eight? Earlier? Later? I don't know now I'm thinking about it. I didn't have the telly on so can't gauge by the programme. I decided to have a read instead."

"Okay, no worries. Can you tell me a little bit about this story that's been in the news? Sorry if it's painful, but it's important we know what's going on from someone close to it."

Nancy visibly relaxed at that, her shoulders lowering, and she splayed her hands on the table, smoothing imaginary swells in the white tablecloth. Maybe she thought that was why Bethany and Mike were there, to discuss the latest news.

"She works at the private abortion clinic," Nancy said. "A young girl came in for a termination, and she died while Opal was operating. It was only Opal's second procedure, and she thought it was her fault, that she'd done something wrong. The other surgeon, who'd stood by watching, told her she'd done it by the book and not to worry. But she went through the mill, I can tell you. Guilt is an awful thing, isn't it? Eats away at you something chronic. It got to Opal so much, I'm surprised there's anything of her left."

There isn't much. Bethany winced.

"Anyway," Nancy went on, "turns out, when they did the post-mortem, the girl had a bad heart. Something about a hole in it? Well, that cleared up any blame, but the press . . ." She worried her bottom lip with stubby front teeth. "A journalist kept bothering her, going to her house, waiting outside, following her to work, that kind of thing. That's a lot to cope with."

Bethany poured boiled water in the mugs, her have-we-got-a-lead radar going off regarding the journalist. Could it be him? "His name?"

"Peter Uxbridge. A right pushy fella. I said to our Opal, I said: You need to ring the police about him. That's harassment, that is. She wouldn't have any of it, though. Said it would die down eventually, but I think she said that more for my benefit, to stop me fretting."

Bethany finished making the tea, giving each one a quick stir. "What was the girl's name — the one who had the abortion? Do you know?"

"Chelsea Bishway."

Oh my God . . .

Nancy sighed. "The poor thing was only fifteen. Her dad was raging in the paper, saying all sorts. Like she wouldn't have had sex voluntarily, if you catch my drift. Some dads can't handle knowing their daughters are growing up fast, can they, so they make up rubbish like that."

Bethany had to have been living under a rock not to have heard chatter about this going around the station, unless it had only been blown out of proportion in the news and hadn't even warranted anything except a few questions to Opal by uniforms. She'd have to check that. She took Nancy's mug over and placed it on a silver coaster. Sitting opposite, Mike standing by the door, she asked, "Do you know if anyone would have been upset enough about this to hurt Opal?"

Nancy nodded vigorously. "I should say so, which is why I've been so bloody worried. I told her to come and stay here for a bit, but she wouldn't. The amount of people who've shouted at her in the street, calling her a baby killer . . . Lots of spite flying around." She sipped her tea.

"Did she have many threats?"

"Like I said, folks shouting at her — random strangers, can you believe — and no one would have known who she was if that nasty Peter Uxbridge hadn't taken a picture of her and put that and her name in *The Shadwell Herald.* I have to say, if I ever see that man . . . well, I won't tell you what I'd do because you're a police officer."

"I can well imagine, Mrs Forrester, but I'd advise you not to take matters into your own hands. Now, I have some distressing news for you."

Nancy scraped her chair back and shot to her feet. "No . . ."

She must have read Bethany's face, fainting before another word had been spoken.

CHAPTER ELEVEN

T shoved Chelsea into the wardrobe then got in there with her. Dad was having a bad day, and Chelsea had spilt some paint by accident. Dad was decorating the living room, and she'd gone in there to get her science book, her foot tapping the paint tray, which had upended on the carpet. Dad was in the shed so hadn't seen who'd done it, but he'd spot it as soon as he came in, so it was best to hide now. If they got lucky, Dad would rant and rave, get all his anger out before he found them. The problem was, it could go the other way. While he searched for them, the anger could mount.

"I'm so sorry, T," she whispered, her little voice reedy and thin. "I didn't see . . ."

He put his arm around her shoulder, one of Mum's shoe heels digging into his bum. "It was easy done. A bit silly of him not to have put a sheet down or something."

"He's going to go mad," she said.

"He will, but don't worry, I'll say it was me." Like he always did. Better that he have the bruises — or broken fingers from Dad squeezing them so hard.

"I hate you taking the blame."

"I won't allow the alternative, you know that."

So they huddled and waited, their breaths harsh, the wardrobe heating up from their sweating bodies. There was limited space — he was 'growing like a weed', so their next-door neighbour had said — and their sides and thighs pressed against each other.

He sang Hush Little Baby *to her, like he always did when they were scared.*

The back door creaked — it needed WD40 — alerting T to the fact Dad had come back inside. T's heart picked up the pace, and his chest hurt, his throat, too, where a lump formed. The carpet was relatively new, and Dad was going to go mental.

"What the fuck?" the man in question shouted, his voice carrying through the ceiling and up the stairs.

Chelsea whimpered. T tightened his hold on her.

"Shh. It'll be okay." He was telling himself that, as well as her.

"But it won't . . ."

"Keep quiet. He's coming up."

Footsteps thundered, Dad shouting, "Where the fuck are you? T? Come out here now!"

Pain streaked across T's chest — a panic attack was on the way if he didn't control his emotions.

The bedroom floorboard groaned — Dad was standing just inside the doorway then. T closed his eyes, willing him to go away. To be nice instead of always annoyed.

"Who the fuck spilt that paint?" Dad raged. "One of you bloody did it, because it certainly wasn't me. Christ, I need you two like I need a hole in the head."

I'll put a hole in yours one day, you bastard.

Chelsea shot up and out of the wardrobe, going too fast for T to hold her back. Light sprawled inside, blinding T for a moment, and he blinked to focus. Chelsea stood in the middle of the room, facing Dad.

"It was me," she said, lifting her foot.

Paint streaked her school shoe.

"You fucking little bitch," Dad roared, taking a step closer, fist cocked.

T lunged out of the wardrobe just in time to get in the way and for the punch to land on his face. It hurt — fuck, it hurt — but he'd take as much punishment as Dad wanted to mete out if it meant Chelsea wouldn't have to know how it felt. T staggered back into Chelsea, and they both went down, T landing on top of her. He scrambled to his feet, pushed out his chest, and waited for more.

Dad stared, eyes blazing, nostrils flapping as he breathed heavily.

"It was me," T said. "I nudged her, and her foot tapped the paint."

"It's always you," Dad snarled. He grabbed T's hand and squeezed the fingers, his face going red. "These have not long healed, yet here we are again."

His sour breath gusted over T's face.

How many times was this man going to break his fingers? How often did he think he could get away with it? T wasn't allowed to go to the hospital, he had to suffer in silence, and Dad only ever clamped on the left hand, so T could still write, cook, and do the housework.

T closed his eyes, channelling out the hurt, going to that empty space in his head where none of this was happening and they lived in a loving home, a peaceful home, not one with emotional time bombs ticking, waiting to go off, exploding in your face. Mum was too far gone to step up and make a stand — she sported black eyes most days. And T thought then, that if Mum couldn't leave Dad for herself, she could at least leave for her children.

Anger roiled inside him, pulling him out of that serene place, and he snapped his eyes open. Stared Dad right in the eye. And kneed him in the bollocks.

The grip on T's hand disappeared, and Dad bent over, grunting.

"Don't you fucking touch me again," T said, suddenly fearless, watching that big, brawny man brought down by a jab to his dick. "If you do, I'm going to the police, got it?" He was seventeen now and buggered if he was going to put up with this bollocks.

Dad straightened. Laughed. But he took a step back.

A victory for T.

"You wouldn't dare." Dad's face morphed into his usual sneer.

"Try me," T said. "Just fucking try me."

* * *

T blinked the memory away. It fuelled his hatred yet also swamped him, and he felt as though he was back there, that kid who'd taken and taken the hits and abuse until he couldn't do it anymore. A snap of time, a glimpse of the past, and everything went to shit.

His eyes burned, and he stared at the cupboard in his room where he hung his clothes. No, he wasn't going to go in there and hide. There was no one to hide from anymore — his dad never came around here. He'd moved out of the family home as soon as Chelsea had died. *This* was home now, a new space, a rented room in a house where two others shared the bathroom and kitchen, but it was better than being *there*, with *him* and *her*. He'd asked if he could put their old green phone in the living room here, though. That thing was a symbol, had always been there in his childhood, asking him in the past to lift the receiver and call the police on his father, call the social services on him and his mother. It reminded him he'd been weak, had suffered because he hadn't had the balls to open his mouth, and pushed him never to accept that sort of thing again.

Mum hadn't reacted at all when he'd gone, but like he'd told her, he had to leave, couldn't stand seeing her in that bed any longer or his bastard father pretending to cry over the loss of his daughter, a child he didn't care much for in life, so why the big deal now? He'd sold a story to *The Shadwell Herald* — what a despicable twat — and accepted money, *money* for a trumped-up tale of woe that was false, all lies.

To take his mind off it, T thought about Opal. How he'd hoovered her insides out, another symbol — cleaning up the mess she made in T's life. He rocked on his bed, grasping his hair, pulling at it as if that would erase everything, his whole life, taking him back to the day of birth where he had a different dad who was proud of him and called him 'son' instead of T for Twazzock.

God, how it all burned. Hurt. Wrenched at his heart.

No one else was in, the other two house-sharers out at work, so he went downstairs to the living room and lifted the phone handset. Dialled. Held his breath.

"Hello?" Her voice was thick, deep with emotion.

He guessed she'd been told about Opal. "Good day to you. I'm calling from Bishway Solutions, and I'd like to offer you a free trial for justice served—"

"Who?"

"Bishway Solutions."

"I'm . . . I can't . . . I don't want to talk right now."

"Oh, but you must."

"I can't. My daughter . . ."

"Bishway Solutions offers you peace in your sort of situation. Eternal peace."

"Please, I just . . . Oh God, please, go away."

"No. No, I won't."

He marvelled at how the people he phoned didn't twig he was using his actual surname in Bishway Solutions. If they told on him, he'd be found in an instant. Maybe that was why he used it. To test fate.

He lowered the handset to the phone and smiled, twirling the coiled line between his fingers. In a moment, he'd call her again, speaking in that cold voice he'd adopted. And he'd ring and ring until she was a mess. Once she was suitably wrecked, he'd go and end it for her.

He was nice like that.

CHAPTER TWELVE

A quick lunch with the team in the incident room gave them all a well-deserved break. Fran mentioned how her daughter had just started walking, and it got Bethany thinking about her lack of children. She'd told Vinny right from the start she wasn't interested, and he'd said he felt the same way, but something inside her yearned, and she wasn't sure how she felt about it.

Maybe one day they'd start a family. Just not yet, when their jobs were dangerous and either one of them could be taken at any minute. Who knew how they'd feel in the future?

Thinking of Vinny brought on a pang of longing, to be with him, to hold his hand, so she excused herself and retreated to her office. She gave him a ring, and he answered, sounding groggy. Probably getting some sleep in. He was on the night shift later. She kicked herself for not remembering.

"Hi," she said. "Sorry if I woke you, I forgot you might be kipping."

"It's okay. I can always nod off again this afternoon."

"How are you feeling?"

"Better. I just need to accept that in my line of work, not everyone is going to come out of it alive."

They chatted for a while longer, and once she was sure he sounded chipper, she went back to the incident room, her heart with Vinny but her head in the game.

"Right," she said, standing in front of the whiteboards. "We have Jason Holt, killed for no apparent reason. We have our theories, but do they really hold water? An affair — could the bit on the side's father have found out and went off the rails? Bear in mind this is if she's underage. Could Georgia have done it? Okay, she was at work, we have confirmation of that from the hospital, but did she get someone else to do the murder?"

She glanced at the image of Jason. "Or did Warren have anything to do with this? Does he harbour a secret love for Georgia? *Does* he, in fact, know all about the affair but lied to us, saying he didn't? Could he have committed the murder then got back down to Cornwall in time?" She shook her head. "That's stretching things a bit. Leona, did you check his alibi at The Blue Anchor Inn?"

Leona nodded. "I did. He was there from seven until closing time. He didn't use his phone, just sat there drinking. Chatted with the manager on and off between customers. They're mates, apparently."

"Bollocks, that's that down the shitter then." Bethany rubbed her forehead. "Okay, it might not have been him, but again, he could have arranged for someone to do it. Do I sound like I'm clutching at straws here?"

"A bit," Fran said, softening the words with a smile. "Especially when there's another option staring us in the face. What about Chelsea Bishway being the other 'woman'? It fits, doesn't it — her being younger, Sam King thinking she was underage. Then she gets pregnant, has to have an abortion, dies, and someone found out she was seeing Jason, then things got out of hand and Jason was killed."

"Then there's Opal Forrester, the one who did the abortion," Leona said. "The link is too obvious to ignore."

Bethany nodded. She'd come to the same conclusion. "It's looking likely, isn't it. Mike, we'll need to speak to that journalist, then go and see Chelsea Bishway's parents."

"I found another news article," Leona said, clicking her mouse and bringing a window up on her screen. *The Shadwell Herald* was in fancy red font at the top. "Seems like the dad went to the press to tell his story three days ago. A broken-hearted man, by all accounts. I feel well sorry for him."

"Then we'll have to tread carefully, but broken-hearted or not, if he has anything to do with this . . ." She walked over to Leona's desk and read the article.

TEEN DEATH HAS CRUSHED FATHER
PETER UXBRIDGE

The death of Chelsea Bishway has come as a huge shock to her family. Her father, William, has talked to us at *The Shadwell Herald* to urge people to keep a closer eye on their children in relation to health.

"I had no idea she had a problem," he said. "She was like any other teenager. To find out she had a hole in her heart was devastating."

Mr Bishway feels that if any parent is worried, to go and get help from a doctor.

The problem is, if children are presenting as being well, why would a parent worry? Like Mr Bishway, they would continue life as normal until the child showed signs of having something wrong, wouldn't they?

When asked that very question, he said, "Get them checked anyway."

With the huge strain on the NHS at the moment, it's not an advisable step to get your child checked if nothing untoward is apparent.

Mr Bishway declined to go into any detail when asked about his daughter's pregnancy; neither did he wish to comment about the private termination clinic or where Chelsea had found the money to have the operation.

"I'm just heartbroken," he said. "That's too much for you to ask of me. Can't I grieve in peace?"

I'm just wondering, if he wants to grieve in peace, why he contacted us for an interview.

* * *

Bethany sighed. Uxbridge was in it for sensationalism, not as a genuine man wanting to help a mourning father. His last line was scathing, bitchy. "Come on, Mike, we'll go and see Uxbridge."

She read the Bishway's address off the board then left the room with Mike, and they got in the car. Bethany opened her window to let in some air, although it was so hot, it wouldn't make a difference until they were on the move. Engine rumbling, she peeled out of her spot and onto the road, heading to the *Herald's* office a short distance away.

Mike scratched his head. "Do you reckon it's Chelsea's dad?"

"It's a possibility, but there are so many variables. Let's keep everything in mind until we have something more concrete to go on. I'd hate to burst into the Bishway's house with an attitude and bring more upset on the poor man. He only buried his daughter last week, so things will still be raw."

"What I can't get my head around is the fact that he spoke to the papers when, like you said, she'd only just been buried. Isn't that a bit off?"

Bethany shrugged. "Some people deal with things in a different way to what you'd expect. What if he's got fire in him to right the wrongs? What if that's his focus, to save other kids? Isn't it better for him to have some sort of direction than not?"

"I see what you mean. Park just there, look. Two spaces, take your pick."

She veered into one of the spots, which was thankfully shaded by the height of the building, the sun behind it unable to splash its wicked heat onto the street. At least the car wouldn't be boiling when they got back in it.

Outside the *Herald* office, she took a deep breath, readying herself to talk to Peter Uxbridge. Would he be his usual belligerent self? More so because tempers frayed in this sort of weather? Whatever, she needed to speak to him, and putting it off wouldn't help solve this bloody case.

They stepped inside the cool interior and approached the desk. A woman sat behind it, typing away, earphones jammed in, tinny music filtering out. Bethany glanced at the name plaque sitting beside the phone — Jade — and waved her hand under the receptionist's nose.

Jade snapped her head up, blushed, and removed the earbuds. "Sorry about that. I got carried away."

Bethany showed her ID. "Peter Uxbridge in?"

"He is actually, but he'll be going out again in about twenty minutes."

"We need to see him."

"I'll just check if he's available."

"He needs to be." Bethany smiled tightly. "Murder enquiry."

"Oh, well, yes, he does need to see you then." Jade jabbed a few numbers on the phone. "The police are here. Right. Yes. Okay." She covered the mouthpiece with her palm. "He said he'll nip to the station later."

"Uh, no. We'll see him *now*."

Jade smiled brightly, as though she enjoyed the thought of telling Peter that. Lowering her hand so he'd hear her, she said, "Peter, it has to be now." She blinked and held the phone out, away from her ear, then stared at it, smirking.

"For fucking hell's bloody sake!" Peter's voice sounded faint, streaking out of the phone in a burst of anger.

Jade pressed it back to her ear. "Someone piss on your cornflakes, did they, dear?" She folded her lips over her teeth and held in laughter, her cheeks flushing. "Yes, of course I'm aware of what I just said. You're not royalty, mate. You're not someone I have to mind my manners with. Take my advice and enrol in a course on meditation to calm you down. You need it." She dropped the handset into the cradle and let out a giggle. "As you've probably realised, he's not in a good mood, but when is he ever? First floor, second door on the right."

Bethany led the way upstairs and waited for Mike to catch up outside Peter's door. She knocked on the opaque glass panel, and a grumpy "Come in!" had her hackles going up. She pushed inside and stood in front of his desk, glaring at the weasel-faced prat who stared up at her with a look of affront.

"What do you want?" he said. "I'm a busy man."

"Busy annoying people with your sub-par stories?" she asked, taking a seat while Mike stood leaning against the wall beside the door.

"Rude." Peter shook his head. "Out with it. I haven't got all day."

She didn't want to give him too much information, but how could she not when her questions related to not only Chelsea Bishway's death but also Jason Holt's and Opal Forrester's? Journalist that he was, he'd run with the new nuggets and let the whole city know some nutter was out there killing people. She'd keep the manner of death to herself. The holes in their stomachs, the skull images, everything.

"I haven't got all day either, Mr Uxbridge, and if I could get away with not talking to you, I would, believe me, but you could be quite significant in our enquiries, so unfortunately, I'll have to suffer your presence and you'll have to suffer ours — for as long as it takes for me to be satisfied, got it?" God, she sounded as though she had a rod up her arse, but this man did her head in, had done since the first time she'd dealt with him a few years ago.

He bristled, his shoulders rising one after the other on repeat, like he was doing some kind of indignance dance.

Such a twat.

"What enquiry?" His eyebrows stretched upwards.

He had green sleepy dust clinging to one of his eyelashes, and she wanted to heave.

"Murder." She waited for a heartbeat. "Now, I want to talk about Chelsea Bishway."

"What about her?"

She resisted rolling her eyes. He clearly had a mind to make this difficult. "Did you find out anything that you didn't include in your articles?"

"What, like she was shagging some bloke much older than her? Yeah, I found that out, although who he is . . . anyone's guess, that."

Great. "Where did you find this information?"

"What, you want me to make your job easier? Shouldn't you be doing the legwork, seeing as it's what you get paid for?"

"Do I need to remind you, Mr Uxbridge, that I could view this as you withholding information and perverting the course of justice? I mean, if I'm trying to find justice, and you're not answering my questions to enable me to do that . . ."

"All right, all right, keep your bloody hair on." The sleepy dust fell and bounced off his cheek, then out of sight. "I asked her friends."

Bethany almost shouted at him but reined herself in. "You questioned *minors*?"

He shrugged. "It was just a bit of a chat, nothing to get your knickers in a twist over."

"Their parents should have been present. You should have asked for permission."

"What, when I'm just gassing to them outside the school, finding out about their mate? Look, it was by the school fence, near where the flowers have been left. Loads of them, there are, carnations, roses, the lot. Plenty of people, too. Parents and the like. I was standing there, minding my own, and heard two of her friends talking. One said, and I quote: I wonder if her boyfriend knows she's dead? So I said to myself, hey up, mate, there's a lead there. So I outright asked them who her boyfriend was. Like I said, they didn't know, Chelsea had kept it secret, but they *did* say he was older than her. A lot older."

Bethany's stomach spasmed. Jason Holt. It had to be.

"Anyway, why is Chelsea Bishway's death now a murder? She had a heart condition; she died because of it. Actually, the anaesthetic caused it — too hard on the ticker."

"It's not Chelsea's death we're investigating." That was all she was prepared to give him. "Did you find out anything else?"

"Not Chelsea's death? Whose is it then?"

"Please answer my question."

"Yeah, that her dad is angry because of it, and her mum's apparently loopy, although that happened way before her daughter died."

"Did her father say anything off the record? I have read your news report, if you can call it that. I have to say, it wasn't your finest."

He snorted. "Yes, he said stuff off the record. Like how he was going to murder the 'son of a bitch' who'd got her up the duff and also the 'cow' at the abortion clinic."

Shit.

Bethany successfully held off a gasp.

They had a so-called heartbroken father to see, one who'd openly admitted he was willing to murder.

CHAPTER THIRTEEN

William Bishway was a stout bugger, the tops of his arms as big as Bethany's size sixteen thighs. He looked about fifty, bald as a coot, Popeye without the pipe, and even had the anchor tattoo on both biceps. A sailor, or was it for some other reason?

He stared at her on his doorstep, grey stubble creating the illusion of a dusting of snow, at odds with the overly warm day. It looked so real, she waited for it to melt. Curly salt-and-pepper hairs peeked over the neckline of his white vest.

"Yeah?" he said, gruff as anything, bordering on rude the way he sniffed then curled his lips back, showing his chipped teeth.

What a catch!

She held her ID up. "DI Bethany Smith and DS Mike Wilkins. We need to speak to you about Chelsea."

"Why? There was no crime in her death, unless you're here about that fucking paedo. Now *that's* a crime. Come in, will you? That sun's burning the top of my bloody head."

They followed him inside. He took them into the living room, where he plonked down on a brown recliner. The space was stuffy, despite a fan whirring. All it did was move stale air around.

"Park your arse." He gestured to the sofa with a banana-like finger. "Want a drink, do you?"

Bethany shook her head. "No, thank you."

"I'm fine, thanks," Mike said, nodding then getting his notebook and pen out. He appeared ill at ease. Was he sensing something?

They sat, and Bethany glanced over at Mike to catch his attention. He made eye contact and frowned, his way of saying: *Something's up.*

"Mr Bishway, we're here to ask some questions as we think Chelsea is related to a murder enquiry we're currently working on."

"You what?" he all but shouted.

I thought only spinach got Popeye going.

"She wouldn't be involved in nothing like that." He cracked his knuckles.

An inkling as to his state of mind?

"No, we don't think she was," she said. "What I mean is, two people have died, and one of the people, at least, has a direct link to your daughter." She waited for his reaction.

"Who?" He sat up straighter, not a sign of guilt on his face.

Genuine or good at hiding it?

She readied herself to speak the words that might change everything. "Opal Forrester."

"Ah, that bitch." He waved as though Opal's death meant nothing. "No sympathy. I hope whoever did her in gave her pain. And lots of it."

"It wasn't Miss Forrester's fault that Chelsea died," Bethany said.

"I know, but it's people like her, who work in them sort of outfits, well, if they didn't exist, Chelsea wouldn't have died, would she."

This man wasn't seeing both sides of the story. Or he knew it but refused to acknowledge it.

"If Chelsea hadn't got pregnant in the first place, she wouldn't have needed the use of such a service." She let the words loiter between them for a moment, then pressed on. "Regardless of how you feel about Miss Forrester, she didn't deserve what happened to her. She was just doing her job. Do you know anything about her death?"

"No, I bleedin' well don't," he said, slapping a hand on the chair arm. The noise echoed for a second, then the fan swallowed it up. His biceps bulged, and the tattoos rippled.

"What do those tattoos represent?"

"Things that anchor me down. I've got another one on my arse. Want to see it?"

She ignored the offer. "What things?"

"None of your damn business!"

"Where were you last night?" she asked, moving to the edge of the sofa. It was uncomfortable — a spring had been poking her backside.

"Oh, so it's come to that, has it? Bloody typical."

"We're aware that you voiced the fact that you would kill the man who got Chelsea pregnant, as well as the woman who performed the termination."

Let's see if he denies it.

"Oh, that reporter bloke has a big mouth. Not surprised. His article didn't have half of what I said in it. And as for saying about killing them, I blurted that in the heat of the moment, that's all. Nothing sinister about it. It's what you say, isn't it?"

Bethany had to agree with him there. The amount of times she'd heard *I'll kill you in a minute* and no one had actually done it. "So, I'll ask again. Where were you?"

"I was here with the wife."

"Where's your wife now, Mr Bishway?"

"Having a bit of a kip. She's worn out from crying. Hasn't stopped since Chelsea died." He grimaced as though that got on his nellies.

"I'd like to speak to her in a moment."

"No need for that. Leave her be."

"I'm afraid there *is* a need. I have to confirm your alibi." She stood.

"Alibi for what? Killing that Opal woman?" He laughed. "Good luck pinning that on me."

"I'll just go up now."

He made to rise.

She held out her hand, palm facing him. "No, don't bother yourself with showing me the way. I'll find it." She left the room and climbed the stairs, then opened the only closed door. "Mrs Bishway?"

The drawn curtains kept the sun out bar strips around the edges. A shaft to the left speared light onto the bed, a slice of brightness on the burgundy cover. The room had the scent of a place never aired, fusty and gag-inducing. Unwashed bodies and bad breath. The woman was on her side, beneath the quilt, her eyes wide and red-rimmed.

A quilt in this heat?

"Mrs Bishway, I'm DI Bethany Smith, and I need to ask you a couple of questions."

"What . . . what about?" Mrs Bishway sat up, her wispy brunette hair bedraggled, a bird's nest on one side, her eye . . . oh.

"Where did you get that bruise on your face?" Bethany asked, instantly on alert.

"I-I walked into the wall."

A likely story.

Bethany went inside and closed the door, wishing she hadn't when the smell intensified. She sat on the edge of the bed, the aroma of manky sheets wafting up. "What's your name, love?"

"Harriet."

"Okay, Harriet, do you need any help?" She took her hand and squeezed it.

"Don't do that," Harriet shouted and wrenched her hand away. "Don't you ever squeeze anyone's hand like that again, do you understand?"

What the eff? "All right. Let's try once more, shall we? Here, just hold my hand. I won't squeeze, I promise."

Harriet tentatively obeyed. Her skin was smooth, as if she hadn't done a day's work in her life.

"There. It's fine, see?" Bethany smiled. "Why mustn't I squeeze hands?"

"*He* does that. It hurts. Breaks fingers. So many times." She closed her eyes for a moment.

Breaks fingers? Fucking hell! "Who is *he*?" Although she suspected she already knew.

"*Him.*" Harriet opened her eyes again, just enough to make slits.

"Do you want to talk about what he does to hands?"

"No." She rocked from side to side and hummed a tune that sounded like *Hush Little Baby*.

Was she talking about William? Was he the one who'd given her the black eye? Who else could have done it?

"That's fine." Bethany would have to leave it for the moment and talk about her main reason for being there. "Where was your husband last night?"

She hesitated, then, "Out at the pub. Always at the pub or round *her* house . . ."

"Who is her?"

"*Her.* He thinks I don't know. Thinks I can't hear them through the wall. Years, it's been."

Sounds like William's been naughty.

"Are you sure he was at the pub?"

"Of course I am."

"So he definitely wasn't at home?"

"No, he came back and . . ." She raised her free arm and fluttered her fingers by her bruised eye, speaking without words as to what he'd done to her.

The lying bastard said he was home. "I see. What time did he come back?"

"About eleven."

It could have been him, given the timeline Presley gave us. He could have killed Opal earlier, then rushed back here.

"Was he drunk when he returned?"

"Yes."

"How drunk?"

"Like he'd had a fair few whiskeys. Maybe half a bottle. That kind of drunk." Her bottom lip wobbled, and she had a shifty look in her eye.

"Which pub does he use?"

"The Fiddler's Bow."

"Thank you."

"If T was here, he'd bring me a cup of tea."

"Who is T?"

"No one." She gazed around as though off her tits on drugs. "He's absolutely no one at all. Nothing to me. Nothing . . ."

"Are you taking medication, Harriet?" Bethany eyed the bedside cabinet. Blister packs of pills. It was too murky to read the wording to know what they were.

"Yes."

"Do you know who Chelsea's boyfriend was?"

She nodded then changed it to a head shake, as if doing that would rub out the first gesture. "Mustn't say." Her eyes flickered from side to side, then she stared at the door. Waiting for William to appear?

"Why mustn't you say?" Bethany pushed.

"I promised Chelsea I'd keep the secret. She said she had no one else to turn to except me and T. She should have just told T. I didn't want to know."

"But Chelsea is gone, love, and I need to know the name of the man she was seeing — he's someone we have to speak to. If he's older than her, we may be able to press charges regarding sex with a minor. If the CPS think he's a risk to other girls, we can stop him, do you see?" That was all she could think of to say, something that would make her want to stop another girl being taken advantage of, even though the man in question was dead. Still, she needed a name to confirm it.

Harriet nodded. "Don't tell *him* I told you. He'll kill him if he finds out his name. He said he would. I heard him tell Mr Uxbridge. Maybe he'll kill me next. Hush little baby, don't say a word . . ."

What the bloody hell? "The name, Mrs Bishway?"

"Jason Holt," she whispered.

Even though Bethany had wanted it to be him, had expected that answer to come from Harriet's mouth, it still sent her mind reeling, her heart racing. The link between Jason and Opal was definitely Chelsea, but the question now was: Did William kill them?

She settled Harriet back down then left her to return to the living room, glad of the marginally fresher air. She paused in the hallway, listening to William gabble on.

"Whoever got her pregnant must have raped her. She wouldn't have done anything like that until she was older," he said.

Bethany thought of Georgia's description, how she'd found Chelsea and Jason in the bungalow. There was no way that girl didn't know what she was doing.

She entered the room and remained standing. "Why did you lie to me, Mr Bishway?"

"I don't know what you're on about," he blustered, cheeks reddening.

"Your wife said you were at the pub last night." She might get Harriet a good hiding for saying that, but she had a job to do, and finding out where William had been was of prime importance.

"She's got her evenings mixed up, hasn't she. That was the other night. She's so doped up on them pills, she doesn't know what she's saying."

"So you didn't come home drunk then?"

He laughed, although his face didn't reflect that mirth. He was angry. Livid. "Drunk? You're having a laugh."

"No, I'm not. How did she get her black eye?"

"Banged it on the newel post most probably, the clumsy mare." He scratched his snow beard.

"Who is T?"

His jaw firmed, and he bared his clenched teeth. "That's my son, although he's no longer a son of mine. He fucked off straight after Chelsea died. Said there was no point in hanging about if she wasn't around. I said to him: What about your mother? And d'you know what he said, the cheeky bleeder?"

"No. Tell me."

"He said she hadn't cared enough about him or Chelsea, so why should he care about her? Or me, for that matter." He sucked his lower lip. "Damn ungrateful little bastard."

"What's his proper name?" she asked.

"Timothy."

"Where did he go?"

"No bloody idea. Don't care."

"Where does he work?"

"Can't remember."

Bethany walked out and stomped upstairs, flinging open the bedroom door, trying not to breathe through her nose. "Harriet, why would your son imply you're a bad mother?"

"Because I am." She laughed.

"If your husband hurts you when we've gone, call me, if you can. I can help you." She placed one of her cards on the bedside cabinet, guessing it would be put in the bin. "Where does Timothy live now?"

"I don't know."

"Where does he work?"

"I don't—"

"Mrs Bishway," Bethany snapped. "It's imperative you tell me."

"At the RSPCA centre," she rushed out.

"Thank you."

She bounded downstairs and stood in front of the man she'd quickly come to detest. "Mr Bishway, we'll be leaving now, but I'll just say that if I find out your wife has hurt her face on a wall or a newel post again, I'll be on your back. If you remember that you were, in fact, in the pub last night, give me a ring. I have no idea why you're lying, but believe me, if it's because you did something to Miss Forrester, I'm coming for you." She flung a card at him then waltzed out.

She sat in the car, fuming.

Mike climbed in. "What the hell got your goat?"

"He's lying."

"I realise that, but we have no proof he was anywhere near Jason or Opal."

"I know, but we're going to find it." She pulled away from the kerb.

"Where are we going?"

"To see some dogs." She crunched into a higher gear.

"Pardon?"

"The RSPCA centre. That's where Timothy works."

"Just how much info did you get out of Mrs Bishway?"

"Enough to gather her husband is a drunken bully. She said she hurt her face on a wall."

"Ah, and he said a newel post."

"Right."

"What else did she say?"

"She told me who Chelsea was seeing."

"Is it who I hope it is?"

"Yep. Jason bloody Holt."

"Christ, do you reckon Mr Bishway is good for the murders?"

"What do you think? He said he was in last night. His wife said he was in the pub and implied he'd bashed her face when he got home. What if he bumped Opal off, went to The Fiddler's Bow, drank enough to get really rat-arsed, then went home so his missus thought he'd been at the boozer all night?"

"We'll nip there after we've been to the RSPCA, yes?"

"Actually, we'll go there now. It's just up ahead, look."

She parked and, inside the pub, collared the manager. Once she'd introduced them and put her ID away, she said, "Do you know a William Bishway?"

"Oh. Him." He tutted and threaded his hands through his black hair. "Yes. He was in here last night giving out his sob story, getting people to buy him drinks. He didn't part with a penny all evening. Always was a scheming sod. Cassandra, that's my barmaid, she was in, too. She'll have seen him."

Bethany's heart sank. "What time did he come in?"

"Seven, and he left about quarter to eleven."

Fuck it. "You're sure he was here *all* night?"

Why is William lying?

"Definitely. I kept my eye on him in case he pissed people off, keep mooching whiskeys off them like he was."

She sighed, loud and long. "Okay, thank you for your time." She stomped out and plonked herself in the driver's seat, eyes glazing over as Mike walked round the car then got in. "Unless that manager is bullshitting . . ."

"I know. Come on, chin up. We have the son to speak to."

"We do. Let's hope he's nicer than his father." She shuddered.

Why were some people such arseholes?

CHAPTER FOURTEEN

The dogs were getting on T's nerves. They barked a lot, overly excited because it was walk time. Many volunteers rolled up daily to help out, and it was T's turn to take Shyla for a run, the Rottweiler that always seemed to want to pull his arm out of the socket. She was shit on the lead, had no training, and rubbed him up the wrong way. Or maybe he was taking his frustrations out on her. She hadn't bugged him until Chelsea had died.

"Stop yanking on the lead, you stupid cow," he snapped at her once he was out of earshot. He preferred exercising her when no one else was around so he could smack the dog if she was naughty — where he couldn't be seen. He shouldn't do it, shouldn't even want to, but it was like a knee-jerk reaction the past few days.

Shyla slowed a bit, probably sensing a wallop was on the way if she didn't.

"That's better. No need for pulling."

He took her down a slope on the centre's grounds, towards the river. It flowed into the city, meeting up with the stretch where he'd dumped Jason's and Opal's innards.

He let Shyla off the lead — one thing she did do well was come back when called — and she gambolled along, happy as

Larry. Guilt pricked at him then. She looked so happy being free to sniff the grass and the reeds wavering in the slight breeze at the water's edge. It wasn't her fault she couldn't behave properly. She'd been treated badly in her last home. Like him. He shouldn't act the way he did either, but he did, and maybe his version of pulling on the lead was murdering people.

"Sorry, girl," he shouted. "I'm sorry I'm so mean to you."

She came running back, tongue lolling, and sat in front of him, gazing up. It seemed like she knew how bad he felt now, for how he'd treated her, and her paw lifted. She cocked her head — waiting for him to take it?

He did, and forgiveness glittered in her eyes.

Why couldn't he be like Shyla? She'd let go of all the times he'd smacked her, ready to start again.

Shit. There was something to learn from this.

He stroked the top of her head, and though she flinched at first, she soon flopped to the grass and bared her belly, a sign of submission.

Tears pricked his eyes at her trust.

"A new page for you and me," he said, ruffling her tummy fur. "I promise."

She got up and barked, as though she'd played once in her old life and wanted him to join her in some fun. He pulled a ball out of his pocket and threw it, and off she went, running along to collect it.

They continued like that for a while, until Shyla panted hard and didn't retrieve the ball so enthusiastically. He headed towards the centre, Shyla on the lead, walking beside him as though she'd never tugged ahead in her life. He patted her back, and when he moved his hand to his side, she licked it.

"Making me feel even worse, are you?" he asked.

He had been no better than Dad, abusing the dog the way he had. Ashamed of himself, he vowed to be more compassionate to all the animals in future.

Not to the people he still wanted to kill, though. They didn't deserve compassion.

As he came to the top of the small rise, he took in the scene — dogs playing, yapping, their walkers smiling and happy. It must be true what they said, that dogs gave you joy. Maybe Shyla would be his salvation.

A man and a woman strode towards him, but they didn't have dogs. The bloke had trousers, a shirt and a tie on, looking all official, while the woman was decked out in a nice pair of jeans and a red blouse. He frowned. Had they come to tell him off for smacking Shyla? Had he been caught on camera or something?

His stomach rolled over.

They stopped in front of him, and he came to a halt, nerves fluttering in his stomach. Shyla sat beside him, huffing.

"Timothy Bishway?" the woman said.

He nodded, even though he hadn't meant to. There was no point in lying. His boss would probably have already told them who he was.

She held up an ID card. "DI Bethany Smith, and this is my partner, DS Mike Wilkins. Can we have a word?"

"What about?" he managed.

"Your sister."

Relief promised to send him to his knees if he didn't watch himself. "I'll just need to put Shyla in her kennel first."

"No, no, it's fine here," she said. "Not like it's going to rain or anything, is it, and the person we spoke to in reception said it would be okay for the dog to stay out a bit longer." She smiled.

He felt even better now. "There are a couple of bench tables over there. Want to sit down?"

She nodded, and he guided them there. They sat opposite him, and he clutched the loop handle of Shyla's lead for comfort. The man, Wilkins, got out a notebook and pen, then gave T the once-over.

T squirmed. The bloke's eyes seemed to see right through him, into the depths of his mind, reading all the secrets stored there.

"What do you need to know?" T asked, thinking he ought to be careful here. What if they knew he'd killed Jason and Opal and were sounding him out, waiting to trip him up? He'd be better off pretending he was sad and had no anger in him towards the pair who'd had a hand in Chelsea dying.

"What are your feelings about where Chelsea was when she died?" Smith asked.

"I felt unhappy that she had to go there." *Put the focus on Dad.* "If she hadn't, Dad would have gone mental."

"He isn't the supportive type then?" A shadow of negative emotion crossed her face — her eyebrows drew down, and her lips thinned.

"That's putting it mildly." T was warming to this. "He didn't treat us too well when we were growing up. Broke my fingers quite a bit by squeezing my hand when he was telling me off."

She sucked in a sharp breath.

Good. He had her sympathy. He held his left hand up, palm facing her, to show her the wonky fingers where they'd healed time and again without splints. "He punched me a fair few times, too, but not Chelsea. I always made sure he got to me instead of her."

"I'm terribly sorry to hear that." She swallowed. "Your mother said Chelsea confided in her and you. About the boyfriend."

"Yeah, and we promised to keep it all quiet, which we did. I feel bad, because it was me who gave her the abortion money, but Dad doesn't know that. Chelsea begged me for help, so I helped. Better she get rid of it — because that's what she wanted — than have Dad start on her, but then look what happened." His eyes itched, and he knuckled the one giving him the most gyp. "If she'd been sixteen, I would have taken her to live with me. I only left once she died — got lucky and found a room in a house."

"You weren't to know she had a hole in her heart," she said kindly.

"No." He shook his head. "None of us did."

"About her boyfriend. What's his name?"

"James Hope, something like that. I know it's a J and H." Had he sounded convincing enough that he didn't know the paedo's proper name?

"Do you know him?"

"No. She said he was coming up to forty, and I told her she shouldn't be with someone that age. They saw each other for a good while. Then he dumped her. She found out she was pregnant. Tried ringing him to let him know, but he never answered. Then she told me and Mum what was going on."

"Do you know an Opal Forrester?"

"Not personally, but she was the poor cow who got all the flack for performing the operation. Not her fault, is it? How was she to know Chelsea's heart was dodgy?" The words turned sour on his tongue. That wasn't what he felt about Forrester at all, but he could hardly come clean on that, could he.

"Where were you last night and the night before?"

He'd known this was coming. The police on TV always suspected family members first. "I was in my new place. On my own."

"How many others share the house?"

"Two. One was out with his girlfriend, the other at work at the pub. I can give you their names if you like."

She nodded.

T gave them, plus his address. Best to seem willing to freely divulge information, although he hoped they wouldn't feel the need to get a warrant to search it. Jason's teeth were in a jam jar at the back of the clothes cupboard. He'd wrenched them out of his fat head, unable to stand seeing his smug grin anymore, even in death. "What do you want to know that for? You know, where I was."

"Jason Holt and Opal Forrester were murdered." She stared at him.

He widened his eyes and hefted air in. "Bloody hell! Who would want to do that?"

"That's what we aim to find out, Mr Bishway." A fly hovered around her, and she flapped it away, clearly irritated. "Are you aware of your mother's black eye?"

That bastard. Then again, there have been times I wanted to punch her myself, what with the way she behaves. "Which one? She had one when I left home, but it was going yellow by then."

"She has a new one. Purple. Black in places."

"It'll be Dad. Likes throwing his fists about, that one. Got a temper on him. It wasn't just me he walloped. He's got a habit of lumping Mum and all, although he was careful never to let me see him doing it."

She closed her eyes momentarily. "Do you know of anyone who would want to kill Mr Holt and Miss Forrester?"

He huffed out a laugh. "Who have we just been talking about? He's the only one I can think of. I'm just glad to be out of there."

"Your father mentioned his tattoos represent things anchoring him down, or words to that effect. Do you know what he means?"

"Us three. Me, Chelsea, and Mum." He held back a shudder. The memory of the time Dad had got inked tried to infiltrate his mind.

"Why would you call your mum a bad mother?"

Someone's been opening their gob. "Because she is." He shrugged, making out none of it bothered him. "She stayed with him. She let him hurt me, bully us. I can't remember a time she wasn't in bed, wallowing in it. Couldn't she have got help? There are plenty of places out there."

"Some women feel they can't leave. Walking out is sometimes harder than suffering the abuse. That may seem ridiculous, but until you've lived with it as an abused spouse, you could never understand. The relationship between a man and a woman is very different to that of a parent and child. A child, like you, may want to get out as soon as possible, but a wife or husband . . . It's complicated. Too much to go into now." She sounded like she recited this often.

"I don't get it. She had kids. That should have been enough for her to break free. Why lounge about in bed all day if you have kids? Why have them in the first place if you're not going to take care of them?"

"Are you angry at them?" Wilkins asked.

T blinked in surprise that the man had actually spoken. "Not anymore. Chelsea dying . . . that took all the anger away. Now I just feel numb. What happened in the past is gone. I can't do anything about it except move along and make sure I don't repeat the abuse on others that I suffered." *Fat chance of that happening.*

"I'm sure you won't. If it makes you feel better," Smith said, "I left my card with your mum and told her to contact me if she wants help."

"She won't leave. If she couldn't leave before she took to her bed, she'll not manage it now. I'm staying out of it. I only hung around for Chelsea, so I could protect her. Mind you, he hasn't hit me for years. Not since I kneed him in the nuts. Fought back. I'd have stayed until she was sixteen, then we'd have both left, started again somewhere else. In a town, a village. Somewhere he wouldn't find us."

"Why didn't you do that when you moved out?" she asked. "Why stay here?"

"Because I still can't leave Chelsea, can I. Who else will look after her grave? Who else will make sure she gets a headstone once the ground has settled? Those two won't bother. Dad won't care, even though he'll make out he does — he's got to look good in front of others — and Mum's got no money. Dad keeps it all." He sighed. Getting this all off his chest was cathartic. "I just . . . I can't leave her, all right?"

"I understand." She patted his fist. "So if your parents aren't bothered, who paid for the funeral?"

Shit, thank God he'd had cash off Jason. "Me. I had savings stashed under my bed."

Shyla flopped onto her side, tongue hanging out.

"I should get this doggy back," he said. "She's knackered."

"Okay. Thank you for your time." Smith rose. "And I'm sorry you had such a hard childhood, I really am."

T stood, and Shyla lumbered upright. "It's not you who should be saying sorry, though, is it."

They walked in a row back to the centre, no words spoken, and T wondered what that meant. He kept his mouth shut so he didn't put his foot in it, but what about them? Maybe they were thinking over what he'd revealed.

Smith said goodbye at the door, and T went inside, conscious of them entering behind him, too, so they could walk through and sign out at the front desk. He didn't look back over his shoulder and instead continued on to the kennel section, where he put Shyla inside then locked the barred door. Her tongue slopped at some fresh water someone had put there while the dogs were being walked, then came to sit in front of the bars. He reached in and stroked her muzzle.

"I'll tell you the whole truth tomorrow, girl, but only you."

She licked his hand then plodded off to her bed, flopping on it and closing her eyes.

"Bye now."

He strode away, hanging her lead up in the equipment room, then got on with the laundry, shoving bed covers and towels in the machine, and it reminded him of his childhood. The washing. The cleaning.

He only had another hour to go, then he could get home and think about tonight.

It paid to watch people. To follow them.

He had an appointment with Opal's mother.

* * *

"You see these?" Dad said, showing off his arms, clingfilm wrapped around the tops, blue ink visible beneath, although what the tattoos were of was a mystery. "They're you two." He pointed at T and Chelsea. "Anchors, that's what you are, right from the minute you were born. Before that even. Holding me back, the pair of you."

T wondered why Dad didn't just fuck off if he didn't want the burden. And why would he want reminders of them being anchors on his arms?

Bloody weirdo.

Dad sat gingerly, wincing. "I had one done on my arse and all. That's your mother, that is. She's as close to my backside as she can be, kissing it, because it deserves to be kissed."

Chelsea blinked a few times, clearly baffled as to why Dad was telling them this, and she was only young so wouldn't understand. This speech wasn't for her benefit, though, but T's. He was used to the barbs, the reminders that he was worthless. That them being conceived was a mistake. Two kids, unwanted by their father, their mother. Her goal was being a lazy cow, when it should be bringing her kids up in a good home.

Bitch.

"Get me a beer, T," Dad said, jabbing at the remote control.

The TV blared to life. T took Chelsea's hand and led her to the kitchen with him, not wanting to leave her alone with that maniac. He took a can of Fosters from the fridge, and it chilled his palm, bringing on a shiver.

"Want to help me hang the washing out?" he asked.

She smiled and nodded. She liked passing him the pegs, and wasn't that just as cute as anything?

He ruffled her hair. "You get it out of the machine and into the basket then, and I'll be back in a sec."

T took the can into the living room, and Dad wasn't sitting anymore. He stood in the middle of the rug, arms bowed at his sides, like T had caught him doing mad exercises or something. But it wasn't that — T knew the stance well.

Dad's fist whacked on T's chin, sending him sprawling backwards into the wall, the beer can going flying, landing with a soft thud on the sofa.

"I hate you," Dad said, then swiped the beer up and tapped the top over and over to stop it frothing when he opened it. "Now fuck off and do your housework like the pansy you are."

T stumbled out and into the hallway, tears coursing, his heart thundering. Why was Mum always in bed? Why did she shy away from what Dad did to them? Why did T have to do all the things a mum usually did?

He hated the pair of them. Dad for his bullying, Mum for the apathy that clung to her, an invisible blanket that encouraged her to remain in its warmth and never break free. Not for herself, not for her kids.

He wiped the tears away and walked into the kitchen, smiling brightly. Chelsea looked up at him, and her lip trembled.

"Did he hit you again?" she whispered.

T nodded.

"What did you do?"

"I don't know." But what he did know was his jaw hurt like mad. "Come on. Let's get that washing hung out so it dries before it gets dark."

He scooped up the basket and led the way into the overgrown garden. That was another job on his list, to mow the grass and weed the flowerbeds.

"My friends, their mums put the washing up," she said, handing him two plastic pink pegs from a row of them she'd made on the table. "I seened them doing it when I went round to play, and they sang as well. Why doesn't our mum do that?"

He wanted to tell her why — that she was lazy, good for nothing, and cared for no one but herself. That she'd chosen to stay out of the way, wallowing in self-pity — or madness. "Because she's not well." The standard answer to explain the woman who did jack shit, blaming it on depression. He wanted to believe it was true, that Mum couldn't help it, but she annoyed him so much with her lack of care for them that he couldn't bring himself to be compassionate anymore.

Why weren't her kids a reason to get up in the morning? Why didn't she love them enough to pack their bags and walk out, a child holding her hand either side of her, off into the sunset of happier days?

"Oh," Chelsea said. "Will she get better one day?" She held out two more pegs.

"I hope so, sis. I hope so."

Another answer swirled in his head: But don't bank on it.

CHAPTER FIFTEEN

"What did you make of him then?" Bethany asked as they entered the incident room. She was hot and sweaty from sitting out in the sun while questioning Timothy Bishway. What she wouldn't give for a cool shower.

"He seems more upset than the parents, I saw that much. Thank God he got away from them. Bloody sad that he felt he had to hang around for his sister's benefit, though. Got to be a good bloke to do that."

"I thought the same." She said hello to Fran and Leona then checked the whiteboards.

Quite a bit had been added, where Fran and Leona had trawled through social media, checked into family members, and had ticked off jobs that needed to be done. Although words were there, they didn't lead to anything. The information was basic — no friends in common for Jason and Opal; Chelsea's cause of death; all three's family members, friends, that sort of thing.

She brought them up to date on the visit to the Bishway's house, The Fiddler's Bow, and the RSPCA centre. "So, what do you think of that?"

"I think the dad's good for it," Leona said. "From what you've said, he sounds like a right angry bastard, and if he hits the wife and has done for years, plus Timothy, too . . . I can't believe I felt sorry for him."

"Hmm. I'm leaning that way myself, that it's him," Bethany said, "but we still need to keep all options open." She pressed her fingertips to her temples. "What's the time?" She glanced at the clock on the wall. "Bloody hell! I thought it was only about three." They had half an hour before calling it a day. "Did anything come of the red contact lenses?" She checked the board again in case she'd missed it. Nope, it wasn't there.

"I'm still working on it," Fran said. "I've been busy on so many things today. I need to update you on them. I haven't had time to write it on the board yet either. I had no idea how many online retailers sold coloured lenses. I'll have to email them all and ask if anyone bought any from them that were sent to Shadwell. We could be talking hundreds of buyers. Apparently, they're quite popular. They're sold in online shops all over the world."

"Let's hope they respond quickly," Bethany said.

"I've made a list of all the online places, plus brick-and-mortar shops, and I wrote a standard letter that I'll just paste in to all the emails."

"Why not just blind copy, saving you the hassle of doing it over and over again? Unless there are too many email addresses, which would mark your mail as spam. So maybe do seven or eight with a few recipients on each." Bethany walked over to the coffee machine to pour them all a drink.

Fran slapped her forehead. "Sometimes I'm so thick!"

"Not at all, you're just overworked. You said yourself you've done lots of poking around today." Bethany filled four cups. "Our brains can only cope with so much at once."

Mike came over and helped add Coffeemate and sugars, then handed out Fran's and Leona's. He took his and slumped into his chair. "My mind is packed. So much information. And the people . . . I keep bouncing from one to the other, wondering who it is." He placed his cup on the desk and counted on his fingers: Georgia, Warren, or Liz Holt

— although none of those three could have actually done it themselves as they have solid alibis; well, we didn't ask Liz where she was, did we?"

"I don't suspect her in the slightest," Bethany said, "but we ought to remedy that, just for the paperwork."

Mike continued. "We also have Sam King — you never know, he could have fancied Georgia and wanted her for himself. Her husband's dead, and there's Sam, ready to swoop in to offer comfort."

"Doesn't explain why he'd kill Opal, though," Leona said.

Mike snorted. "To take the spotlight off him? All right, there's any of the JJ Builders employees. William, Harriet, or Timothy Bishway. Have I forgotten anyone?"

"Opal Forrester's mother," Bethany said, taking her coffee and sitting on a spare desk. "Although I really can't see that myself. Why would she want to kill Jason and her daughter? Doesn't make sense. Same with Liz Holt. She wouldn't want to kill her son, surely, or some woman she doesn't even know. Why would any of them kill both people — apart from the Bishways?"

"What if none of them did it?" Leona asked. "What if it's someone who's yet to appear in the investigation?"

"That's a scary thought." Fran shuddered, turning her back on her monitor. "Okay, the emails have been sent. I suppose the replies will trickle in from tomorrow."

"More than one pair of red contacts would have been bought," Bethany said. "Maybe not in a batch, but one at a time to the same address. Jason and Opal both had them on their eyes — which reminds me, I must check my emails to see if Presley got hold of me. One second . . ."

She looked on her phone. Just a short one from him saying he'd have to write to her tomorrow. He must be having a hard time getting them done. Not surprising. The bodies had been a mess.

She carried on the discussion. "Has this person got someone else on their list? If we think about the scenario here, we might be able to work out who's next if that's where this is going. Jason got Chelsea pregnant. Opal performed a termination on her. Both of them had something to do with Chelsea even *needing* such a procedure. So who else is there involved in that? Doctors? Consultants? A nurse? The anaesthetist? Christ, the list could go on and on."

She turned to write that down on a clean board. "Tomorrow, Fran, Leona, you get talking to everyone who had anything to do with the termination, please. Ringing the clinic will be fine. We're not suspecting any of them at the moment, just asking questions to determine whether we think they're next to have their insides hoovered."

"Don't," Mike said, shaking his head. "I'd got it out of my head until you said that."

"Well, it's back there now. You're welcome." Bethany grinned. "Okay, let's go over this as we know it so far. Sorry if I'm repeating myself, but it's doing my head in. Jason Holt is killed by someone annoyed at his relationship with Chelsea Bishway. This could be any number of people; they all have reasons. Then Opal Forrester is killed, also because of Chelsea Bishway — unless it's a massive coincidence, and I have no money in my purse to buy that. That's our link, I'm sure of it. This person may choose someone else or they may stop as of now. There's a whole scope of people to choose from if they do opt to kill again — far too many for us to send uniforms out to, keeping an eye on them, and also, we may be barking up the wrong tree, and the chief isn't going to be happy at us sending our guys out to guard umpteen people when there might not be any need."

"No, he isn't," Kribbs said.

Bethany turned.

The chief stood in the doorway, leaning on the jamb, arms folded. "Much as I'd like to keep everyone safe, we just don't have the resources. Carry on."

He'd put her off her stride, and she couldn't remember what else she wanted to say. She scanned the whiteboards for inspiration. "Oh yes. We have a long shot going on as to whether the contact lens companies even write back, and then, if they admit they've sent lenses to Shadwell, we'll need to go down the official route in order to get a list of names and addresses off them. That could take days."

Her mobile rang, and she got it out of her pocket. "Isabelle. Excuse me a sec." She swiped the screen. "Hi."

"Just updating you before it's time to go home."

"Let me just put you on speakerphone, all right? We could all do with hearing this, and it saves me repeating it." She selected the function and put the phone on the desk.

Everyone came over to gather round.

"Can you hear me okay?" Isabelle asked.

"Yep."

"Right. The footprint on the bedding at Opal Forrester's. It matches a boot sold in Shoe Zone. We've done the legwork there and got hold of the one in Shadwell — I gathered you'd have your hands full with other things; hope I haven't stepped on any toes. Anyway, they've done a search of those boot sales, and one hundred and sixty-five pairs went out the door in the last six months. One hundred and five paid in cash, which surprised me, seeing as it's a debit and credit card world these days. However, you're going to have to get the paperwork going to wrangle the names of the card buyers out of them. The manager quite rightly wouldn't budge on giving them to us. Also, there's the online shop to deal with."

"I'll sort that in a moment." Kribbs propped a hand on the desk.

"Great," Isabelle said. "Now, the hoover dust receptacle had more than just innards in it — and, by the way, the organs must have been taken away the same as with Jason, as they weren't in the hoover, just fat and flesh."

"What on earth are you talking about?" Kribbs asked, eyes going wide.

"I'll tell you after the call, sir," Bethany said.

Isabelle went on. "It had ripped card in it, the sort small things are stored in, and we pieced it all together this afternoon. Granted, it has a lot of blood on it, but it became clear that it's a little box that contained contact lenses."

"Yes!" Fran said. "What brand?"

"They're called Eye Spectacular," Isabelle informed them. "Online shop based in Liverpool."

"They're on my list," Fran said.

"Brilliant." Bethany sighed out in relief, thankful it wasn't from China or somewhere. The UK they could deal with. "That's going to save us a lot of hassle."

"I'll get the paperwork going for that as well," Kribbs said.

"Why anyone would want to rip the box up into tiny pieces and not just take it away with them is anyone's guess." Isabelle sounded tired. "But people are weird, so there you go. We're still studying the pictures of the blood left at the scenes, working out spatter patterns and whatever. Right-handed from what we've discovered, so that makes this harder. It would have been nice to have a lefty — less folks to narrow down. Anyway, what I found interesting was in Opal's garden, a row of pink pegs had been laid out on the table. A perfect line of them."

Bethany frowned. "What the hell could that mean?" For some reason, she recalled the crystals and jewellery that had been taken from Georgia's room and wrote it down on a pad before she forgot to ask Fran and Leona about it.

"No idea," Isabelle said. "If they were randomly placed, I wouldn't have thought anything of it, but it seemed too deliberate. Thought I'd mention it — might be nothing, might be something. Tomorrow is another day, so we'll continue looking through the images and see if anything else jumps out. Fingerprint results should be back in a day or two."

"Thanks," Bethany said.

Call over, she slid the phone in her pocket. "What about the pawn shops? I didn't see anything on the boards regarding that."

"What's that about?" Kribbs asked.

"Crystals and jewellery stolen from Georgia Holt's bedroom." Leona walked back to her desk and picked up a wad of paper. "I was about to add this to the board before you came in, Beth. No one so far has had anyone coming in to sell these things." She showed Kribbs the items in question. "So I've told them if someone does, to try to get an address off them then ring us."

"Okay." Bethany nodded.

"About the hoover . . . ?" Kribbs raised his eyebrows at Bethany.

"Oh, this is something else, like nothing I've ever seen." She shuddered. "Jason Holt's and Opal Forrester's innards were removed, but the killer decided to *hoover* Opal's midsection for some reason."

"To mimic the suction used in terminations?" Kribbs asked.

"Most probably." Bethany was pissed off she hadn't thought of that. It was such an obvious connection, too. "And maybe that's what the hole being left in the bodies means . . . Too 'out there' to think the killer is showing that Chelsea was being made hollow, as in, her foetus was being taken away?"

"It's possible." Kribbs rubbed his finger across his chin below his bottom lip. "It's something to think about."

"So then we need to work out why the skull image, why the face skinning, why the red eyes?" she said.

"Death?" Kribbs suggested. "The skull, I mean. Maybe it's just that, nothing more. The red eyes could be representative of the Devil, or just evil, a monster. Did they view Jason and Opal as such?"

"Has anyone delved into the skull image?" She looked at Fran then Leona, hoping they hadn't dropped the ball, especially with Kribbs here to witness them admitting they had.

"Yes, don't worry." Fran smiled. "It's on my desk ready to be pinned on the board. Looks like the picture was just lifted off Google. The exact one, complete with red eyes, is on page thirty-six. I followed the link to a site called DeviantArt. A man with the username Ah_Tist_1983 created it. I emailed him — his details were on his DeviantArt profile — and he created it for free: commercial and personal use. Anyone can download and use it, no attribution required."

"So the killer must have printed it off and stuck it on the material," Bethany said.

"I looked up where you can buy kits to create your own T-shirt printing." Fran fiddled with her earlobe, which was bright red. "There's one you can buy that enables you to iron on images, so my guess is they drew the skull on the special transfer paper, cut it out, and did it that way. But . . ."

"God, don't tell me." Bethany sighed. "Loads of online stores."

"Yes, but also one in Shadwell, a printer's shop. I rang the manager, a Lee Topper, and he's only sold two in the last month — one to a man, one to a teenage girl, both paying cash. He has CCTV inside the shop and out, so he's going to sort the files. Said we can pick it up in the morning because he'll be chopping it to the specific times and frames this evening once the shop's shut."

"Fuck that," Bethany said. "We'll go there now. Mike!" She dipped her hand in her pocket to get her car keys out. "If you can just do a tiny bit of research before you go home, girls. Split it between you so it takes less time. I want to know who Chelsea's closest friends were. Seeing as we're going to view CCTV, we need to know what colour hair they've got. A teenage girl bought a printing kit. Could a *kid* have done this as revenge for Chelsea dying?"

Kribbs frowned. "It isn't unlikely, but I'd say we're after an adult here."

"All the same," Bethany said as she sailed out of the room, calling back over her shoulder, "best to check all avenues. We don't want this coming back to bite us on the bum."

CHAPTER SIXTEEN

Perfect Printing stood wedged between a fruit and veg shop and a boutique that sold vintage clothing down a side street off the main centre. The buildings had probably been houses in days gone by, the stone of the outer walls like something from a different era. The windows were bay, formed with small squares, some with bull's-eye panes.

Bethany parked down the road a bit, thankfully entering a space just as someone left it. They headed inside, where a blond man in a navy polo top stood behind a white desk, writing something on a spreadsheet. He slid it to one side once he noticed them.

"Mr Topper?" She raised her ID. "DI Bethany Smith, DS Mike Wilkins. Our colleague rang you earlier about the CCTV. I'm afraid we can't wait until tomorrow. This is a double murder enquiry, so you can imagine we're chomping at the bit to see the tapes. We need you to do it now really."

He scratched his long hipster beard. "Oh, okay. Let me just lock the door. We need to go out the back, and I'd rather not leave the shop empty. No one else is in to take over — they leave at four, and it's . . . well, quarter past five now, so shutting fifteen minutes early won't hurt."

He walked round the desk and to the door, pushed the nub up on the Yale lock, then pulled down the black blind, doing the same on the window, casting the interior into gloom. No lights were on, what with the sun being so bright.

"There we go. If you'd like to come this way."

He led them through a door behind the desk, past a load of printing equipment, to a room at the back. An office — teak desk, black leather chair, and a few filing cabinets. A stack of red plastic chairs stood behind the door, so he took two off and placed them in front of the desk.

"Sorry, they're not the most comfortable."

"It's fine," Bethany said.

Topper sat and wiggled his mouse to activate his screen. "I already sorted the files earlier and put them onto one dongle — I had an hour or so spare that I wasn't expecting — but what I didn't do was watch them. Now, I'm a bit old-fashioned, and as well as keeping digital recordings of sales on the computer, which is connected to the till, I also write it in a ledger, dates and times of purchase, so this will make things much easier. Two secs, and I'll get it. Bloody forgot to bring it in."

He left the room, and Bethany took a gander. Prints in black frames hung on the wall to the left above the filing cabinets. She guessed they were images customers had asked for, or maybe they'd been done to show what the company could do, a visual portfolio on display. Either way, they were good, and she especially liked one with a woman standing with her back to the camera, her red coat striking against the gloomy grey woodland surroundings, a path meandering into the foggy distance. It reminded her of a thriller book cover, minus the typography.

Topper returned and nipped behind his desk, opening the ledger and placing it on the desk so it was upside down to him but easily read by Bethany and Mike. They all sat, and she leant forward, scanning lines of text and numbers in columns: Date, time, cost, purchase, payment method.

"Here," he said, jabbing a fingertip on a date three weeks ago. "The girl bought that. Now, you may think I'm weird for remembering her, but she was unusual and stood out to me. She had long black hair, but when she swished it, turquoise was underneath. I notice things like that — I'm also a photographer and painter — so she stuck in my head. She was about fifteen, had a gold ring in her nose, and a silver bar with balls on each end in her left eyebrow."

"Bloody hell, you're perceptive," Mike said. "We could do with you down the nick."

Topper laughed. "Okay, so she paid with a tenner, and I know that because she had black polish on all but one nail — the thumb was turquoise, matching her hair. The thumb was over the ten on the note, and she had a bit of skin sticking up, as if she'd bitten it. Looked like it'd been bleeding, to be honest."

"What about the man?" Bethany asked.

"Well, he's a week ago, and he stuck out because he had a hoodie on, the hood up, pulled low over his eyes. I thought: What the hell is he wearing that for in this heat? I was sweating in just this top, even though I had the fan on, so you can imagine he must have been boiling. I couldn't for the life of me work out how old he was. Could have been in his twenties, thirties, or older. He was clean shaven, couldn't see his hair or eyebrows to know what colour they were, and the really odd thing?"

Bethany held her breath.

"He had gloves on." Topper leant back in his chair, clearly pleased at delivering that little snippet. "Who wears gloves in the summer unless you're doing gardening or whatever? Certainly not the type you lot use. Latex things. Cream in colour, slightly transparent. His fingers were crooked, and the nails were weird, like he'd bashed them with a hammer at some point. You know, raised and ridged, lumpy, and they hadn't grown back properly."

The mention of a hammer had Bethany's heart racing. "Notice anything else about him? His accent?"

"He didn't speak. Odd, because most customers like to have a chinwag. I asked him if he was printing anything nice, and he dipped his head even more, shoved a twenty at me, and waited for the change. These are nine ninety-nine, the packs we're talking about. You get several transfer pages inside, so it's a bargain. Let me show you what they're like. I could brain myself for not being more organised. Won't be a minute."

He left the room again, and Mike copied the information from the ledger into his notebook. The girl had purchased at four-fifteen in the afternoon, and the man at nine thirty-two a.m.

"It's sounding like the bloke to me," she said quietly. "Like Topper said, why wear a hoodie and gloves in this weather? Got to be insane — unless you're trying to hide your appearance."

"And you don't want your fingerprints on the printing pack in case you get caught."

"There is that."

Topper's footsteps heralded his imminent arrival, so she nudged Mike with her knee.

"Right," Topper said, standing at the end of his desk. He opened the printing pack, which was about three quarters of a metre long, half wide. "As you can see, there's plenty of space here so you can do multiple prints if they're small, and large ones, say, if you want to do the whole front of a T-shirt or whatever. The sheets in this size pack are only in white."

The skull had been white but the eyes red.

"I just need to send someone a quick message, sorry." She dashed one off to Isabelle, asking her if she had any information on the red eyes on the skull material and: CAN YOU SEE WHETHER THE RED HAS BEEN DRAWN OR PAINTED ON? "Okay." She returned her attention to Topper. "The white of it. Could someone draw red over the top and it'd stay there?"

Topper shrugged. "You know when you buy a ready-made printed top — let's say it has a logo on it, maybe of a lion's head. The T-shirt is black, the lion white. That white stuff is smooth and sort of shiny, right? If you used a felt tip on it, the colour would wash off and would even be smudged by a finger. You'd need to use a biro or paint on it, oil-based paints, and hope it'd stay there, but of course, you risk it coming off in the wash."

She blew out a breath, trying to recall if the red of the eyes was painted or obviously drawn with a pen. No, it had appeared printed to her. "Are there any coloured printing packs available?"

"Yes, but he didn't buy them from me — and they come in a smaller size. All he purchased was this one."

"Could you print on top of the white?"

"Yes, because you need to use a damp cloth for this sort. You put it over the white template you've made and iron it."

"I see what you mean. So, we need to see the tapes."

"Let me just whizz to the time they came into the shop. Who do you want to see first?"

"The man."

Her phone buzzed with a message alert. "Sorry. You carry on."

Topper got on with working on his computer. She accessed her messages. Two.

One from Leona: I GOT HOLD OF THE HEADMISTRESS AT THEIR SCHOOL BEFORE SHE WENT HOME. CHELSEA ONLY HAD TWO CLOSE FRIENDS. LISA CLARKE, EMMA DAVIDSON. BOTH BLONDE.

One from Isabelle: PRINTED, SAME AS THE WHITE SKULL.

She replied thanks to both of them, then got up to stand on the other side of the desk so she could see the monitor. Mike did the same.

"Here we are," Topper said.

The shot was in black and white, but thankfully not grainy. The man entered the shop and browsed the printing packs to the left of the screen. The camera was behind the desk and showed the back of Topper's head. He lifted it for a second, then continued with whatever he was doing.

"I was drawing a logo there on the computer for a client," he said.

The man glanced over, took a small package off the hanger, and slid it up under his hoodie, wedging it inside his waistband.

"That fucker stole something!" Topper sounded mortified. "I can't believe I didn't spot that."

"You were busy. It happens," Bethany said.

"I know, but that's a bloody fiver."

The customer picked up the large printing pack, brought it to the cash desk, and, like Topper had said, kept his head bowed. Did he know there was a camera pointing at him? Had he checked the shop out beforehand so he knew what to wear and what to do? He did indeed have latex gloves on, and he used his right hand to take his wallet out of his pocket and remove the money.

So he'd possibly picked up a pack with red transfer sheets in it and was right-handed. Bethany was giddy with having got somewhere. Even though they couldn't see who he was, it was something. She studied him: bulky, a bit like William Bishway, around the same height as William, Timothy, and Warren Holt. Honestly, at this point, it could be anybody.

He turned after taking his change, and a large Nike tick was on the back of his hoodie. Leaving the shop, he went right.

"You have CCTV outside, yes?" she asked.

"Yes, I'll go to that file now." He did, finding the right time, and pressed PLAY.

The customer walked off up the road, and at the end, melted into the crowd of shoppers in the busy main thoroughfare.

"Okay, we've seen enough now. Thank you."

Topper closed the files and handed her the dongle. "You can keep that." He shook his head. "I still can't get over him nicking off me."

"Do you think you'd know him if he came back in again?" she asked.

"Well, if he's wearing winter clobber and gloves, yes, and also, I'd recognise his mouth and nose. They weren't anything to write home about, just that I'd know them if I saw them again."

"Okay, we need to shoot off now."

They followed him into the shop, and he opened the door. Out in the street, she waited for Topper to lock up again.

"CCTV for the street he disappeared into?" she said.

Mike nodded, and they walked to the end. A camera was on the wall outside H & M, so they went inside and collared the manager. The shop was open until eight tonight, so that was handy. With the CCTV copied onto a disc, they returned to the station, where Bethany shoved it in Mike's computer.

"You sort that to the right time and day while I make us a coffee." She checked the clock. "Bloody quarter past six."

Drinks poured, she joined him at his desk. He played the video, and it showed the man entering the crowd, but then he got lost in a swarm of people crossing the road — he must have ducked down in the middle of them in order to appear out of sight.

"Bastard," she said. "He knows exactly what he's doing."

"He does. Clever. Got it all worked out."

She wrote up the latest findings on the whiteboard, then they sat and drank their coffees. Bethany suddenly realised she wasn't going to get to see Vinny before he went to work. He started at six-thirty, and wasn't that just a twist of bad luck? She had the mad urge to cuddle him so sent a text.

SORRY I DIDN'T GET HOME IN TIME. LOVE YOU.

A reply came straight back.

LOVE YOU, TOO. SLEEP TIGHT.

She sighed and browsed her images, photos of them smiling on holiday in Aruba. It had been a wonderful break, both of them forgetting their difficult jobs and becoming just *them* again, a couple together, in love. She'd have a poke about online and see if there were any cheap late bookings she could snap up. They both had days due, the pair of them rarely able to take time off. Well, that would have to change.

"Do you want to come to mine for a takeaway?" she asked, looking at Mike to see his reaction.

His eyebrows went up in surprise. "That'd be lovely."

"Vinny's on the night shift, so I'm using you really."

He feigned being hurt, clutching his chest.

"Well, he finishes about two in the morning." She shoved his shoulder and laughed at him still dicking about, pretending to sob. "I don't know about you, but I don't fancy sitting there all by myself. You can stay over if you want."

"Yeah, all right. Drop me off home to get some clean clothes, will you?"

"Yep." She shot another message off to Vinny to let him know not to be freaked out when he spotted Mike's shoes by the front door. Mike often stayed over, so it wasn't a problem. "Let's go. Chinese or Indian?"

"Ooh, Indian for me."

They left the station, and Bethany had a feeling they'd talk about the case all night.

CHAPTER SEVENTEEN

Nancy Forrester stared at the TV. Bradley Walsh asked questions on *The Chase,* The Dark Destroyer plugging in his selection pretty sharpish, leaving the poor contestant panicking so she inputted hers too quickly and got it wrong. That was how Nancy felt when answering the cold caller. What if she said the wrong thing and lost whatever game he was playing?

The thing was, Nancy wasn't wholly paying attention to the show, she just caught a glimpse of it every so often. Her mind was mainly with Opal. What were they doing to her body now? Poking at it? Draining it? Washing it?

A family liaison officer had called round earlier. Alice Jacobs, her name was. She'd explained what was going to occur. That Opal had been taken to the morgue, and they'd do a post-mortem on her. Nancy couldn't bear what had happened to her lovely daughter. It was all so wicked, so evil. And she couldn't bear the thought of what that medical examiner was going to do either. Why couldn't they just leave her alone and let her rest in peace?

She sighed, trying to take in the chatter on the TV so her head wasn't filled with gruesome things, but they might as well be talking gibberish for all she understood. How she used to love this programme, but now it would always remind her of this day.

She felt utterly broken.

Would she ever heal?

She doubted it. Nothing would be the same now Opal was gone. She wished she was dead, too.

Nancy's house phone rang, and she near enough crapped her knickers. What if it was that horrible man again? He'd called her while Alice had been here, too, and Nancy had answered it, just in case there were consequences if she didn't. Holding it together and not giving her fear away to Alice was one of the hardest things to do, when all along she'd wanted to let Alice listen so she could help, but he'd once threatened to kill random people if she didn't do as he told her, and she couldn't have that. Nancy had pretended to Alice that it was a friend, and her answers, she hoped, had reflected that. Alice hadn't questioned her afterwards, so Nancy must have succeeded.

She reached for the phone and lifted the handset. She wouldn't speak this time. No, she'd wait to see who it was.

Seconds passed. Breathing came down the line. A grunt. And what sounded like a sniff.

"Well, hello there. I'm calling from Bishway Solutions, and I'd like to offer you a free trial for—"

Her stomach contracted. Those words. They sent fear into her heart.

"Oh God. Please, *please* stop ringing me," she whimpered. "I can't cope with it."

"Can't do that." He laughed, maniacal and so weird. "What are you up to? And don't lie to me. I'll know if you do."

"I'm watching *The Chase*."

"Is that copper bitch still there?" His breathing grew heavier.

"No."

A few taps. His fingertips drumming on something? "Are you telling me the truth, Nancy Pancy?"

"Yes."

"What chaser is it?"

"The Dark Destroyer."

"What about the first contestant? What's their name?"

Nancy squinted to read it. "I haven't got my glasses on, but I think it says Val."

"Okay, I'll let you off. I believe you." He paused. "Where is Georgia? Did you find out for me?"

She had, and she felt so guilty, but he'd said he was going to hurt her if she didn't ask Alice, and if Alice didn't tell her, Nancy was to find out some other way. How, she didn't know, but thankfully, that was no longer a problem. "Yes." She hated that her voice was weak.

"Right. I'll be round soon for you to tell me in person."

Panic fluttered inside her, a billion wasps buzzing in her chest. "Can't I just tell you now? Do you have to come round?" If he arrived on her doorstep, would he kill her, too? Do to her what he'd done to Opal and that other poor man? Maybe it was better if he did. She'd be out of this then, out of the grief.

"No," he snapped. "Face to face, and that's the end of it. Now, carry on watching *The Chase*. I'll be asking questions about it later to make sure you followed my instructions. And remember, you tell the police, and I'll hurt you and others."

"Okay, okay," she said, breathing erratically. "I'll do whatever you say."

"Good. Now piss off and concentrate on the telly."

More of that strange laughter, then the line went dead. Nancy put the receiver down, her hand shaking. She stared at the screen, struggling to hear what they were saying, unable to make head nor tail of it. Fear sent her pulse thudding in her ears, drowning everything out. She willed herself into a calmer state, listening intently, reaching for her specs so she could see clearly.

Bradley asked, "Which gem, the national stone of Australia, is a hydrated amorphous form of silica? Diamond, ruby, or opal?"

Opal.

Nancy wailed and couldn't stop.

* * *

T laughed so hard at the fear in Mrs Forrester's voice. God, it had been a game-changer asking her to find out where Georgia was. He'd nipped by Holt's house after his shift at the centre and realised, with the police still going in and out, that she might not be there. At the end of the street, a couple of women neighbours had stood talking, so he'd stopped the van, opened the window, and asked them what was going on.

"Someone got killed," the blonde had said.

"And the wife's been taken somewhere else," the black-haired lady had added. "Stands to reason. It's a crime scene. I'd be buggered if I'd live there now. It'd give me the creeps."

He'd carried on his way after that, annoyed his plans had been ruined. The police wouldn't be there forever, but he stupidly hadn't figured them moving Georgia elsewhere.

In the living room at his shared house, he'd rung Mrs Forrester.

"Good afternoon. I'm calling from Bishway Solutions, and — "

"I can't talk at the moment, Karen," she'd said. "The police are here about my Opal."

He didn't know how he felt about being called Karen. "Find out where Georgia Holt is. If you don't, I'll chop off your toes."

He just about wet himself now, cracking up about that. He'd gone on to describe, in great detail, how cigar cutters, when sharpened to a high degree, snipped off all the little piggies on a foot quite easily. He reckoned she'd shit herself upon hearing that, and God, he wished he'd been there to see it.

"Okay," she'd assured. "I'll do that."

"Good. If you breathe one word about this call to that copper, your fingers will be next, got it?"

"Yes. Thank you. You're so kind."

He doubled up again remembering the quiver in her words, then the front door slammed shut, and he closed his mouth, sobering fast. The woman he shared with, Cassandra, came into the living room and plonked down on the sofa.

"What a day," she said, her plait sitting on her shoulder, a creepy black snake. "And I've got to go back out in an hour to do my shift at The Fiddler's. They've got a lock-in because of the darts tournament, so I won't be back until gone three, then I've got to get up at eight and start all over again. Running on gas, me."

T clenched his teeth. His dad went to The Fiddler's, always had.

"Sorry about that," he said. "Like they say, no rest for the wicked." He smiled, hoping she took it as a joke. He needed to keep her onside.

"Then I must be *really* wicked, because I have sod all rest except on a Sunday." She grinned, showing her perfect teeth. "What are you up to tonight?" Her plait squirmed.

He shivered, imagining the hair sticking out below the rubber band was a flicking tongue. "I'll be staying in, as usual."

"Ben's off out with his missus, then he's at her place overnight, so you'll have the house to yourself again. To be honest, we're rarely here, as you've probably noticed. Sorry if you wanted to share with people who are around to *bond*." She rolled her eyes.

"Nah, you're all right. I like being by myself."

The situation suited him down to the ground. With neither Cassandra or Ben knowing whether he was in or out most of the time, he could get on with what he needed to do, them none the wiser, and if that Smith and Wilkins came sniffing round to ask them questions, his housemates wouldn't be able to tell them much — not that they'd even be here when the police came calling.

He was safe. So long as he was careful.

* * *

He waited until ten o'clock and, under the cover of a moonless sky, drove to Nancy's street, parking a few houses away so no one would match his vehicle with her murder once news spread of her death. Frightening her with having her fingers and toes chopped off wouldn't stop her opening her mouth to someone in the end, so he'd have to get rid of her. Anyway, she'd given birth to the bitch who'd helped kill Chelsea, so she was doomed by association.

Unlucky for her.

He carried his large holdall containing everything he needed — tools, a plastic box for the innards, a roll of black bags, the skull material, Superglue, a sock, and the hammer. He'd enjoyed embedding the latter in Opal's head and wanted the rush of doing it again. Nothing beat the sound of it cracking bone.

T walked down the alley between her detached house and the next, entering her side gate into her garden. He placed his bag down, put on his latex gloves, and tapped on the back door, staring through the glass into the darkened room. A light came on in the hallway beyond, and a woman appeared in the doorway, staring at him, her face pale, eyes wide, a cigarette stuck to her bottom lip. He took the cigar cutter out of his pocket and held it up, flexing the handles to get his point across: *If you don't let me in, I'll use these on you.*

He was going to use them anyway, but whatever.

She stubbed the fag out in a saucer on the worktop, the dirty baggage, then shuffled over and twisted the key, making eye contact all the while, then pulled the door wide. The smell of new and old smoke wafted out at him. He raised his finger to his lips to keep her quiet, and she nodded over and over, stepping back, scared shitless by the looks of her. He held back laughter and went in, hefting his holdall with him. The damn thing was well heavy.

Locking them in, he gestured for her to walk out of the kitchen and followed her into the living room, turning the light on in there.

"Bishway Solutions at your service," he said, a giggle bubbling in his windpipe.

She backed away to the sofa and lowered onto it. "Please, don't hurt me."

She appeared sufficiently wrecked, like his mother, and he enjoyed seeing it. Mum *needed* to feel wrecked after the life she'd let them live, and this woman here, well, he hoped she rotted in Hell for spawning a murderer.

He thought about his words to Smith, how he'd said it wasn't Opal's fault Chelsea had died — and brushed it away. Thoughts like that didn't belong here, no matter how true they were. Not when he had a job to do. Not when he needed to *do* something to avenge Chelsea's death. Whether it was right or wrong, it didn't matter.

He checked the curtains — closed. Good-oh.

"Tell me one of the answers on *The Chase*," he demanded, squeezing the cutters. He'd had to watch it on catch-up in order to make sure she'd done as he'd told her. While her viewing *The Chase* wasn't needed, he liked the sense of control it gave him, to have someone bend to his will.

"Opal."

"Ah, so you *were* watching it. Where's Georgia?"

"At The Ringer Hotel."

"What room?" He narrowed his eyes at her, wanting to appear menacing.

Her whole body juddered, so he reckoned he'd succeeded.

"I don't know. I tried all ways to get her to slip up, even asked if I could go and see Georgia, but she wasn't having it. Alice wouldn't tell me."

"Alice? Who the fuck is Alice?" He *did* laugh then, the song chanting through his mind. He sang some of it. "Twenty-four years just waiting for a chance . . ." Ironic. He'd suffered twenty-four years of wanting to pay the world back for the life he'd been forced to live.

"What are you talking about?" she asked, wringing her hands, her nails gnarled and ridged.

A bit like his.

"Never you mind. Get on the floor." He pointed for emphasis.

She stared at his gloved hand, shuddered, and sank off the sofa to her knees.

"And take them stupid fucking slippers off."

She loosened them from her feet then kicked them away. "What . . . what are you going to do to me? I did what you wanted. I got the information."

"Shut up, you annoying old bitch. You didn't get *enough* information, and that's narked me." He opened his bag and took the sock out, shoving it in her mouth.

Her lips stretched tight, and it looked as though that hurt. She moved her hand to take it out, eyes bulging.

He flexed the cigar clipper handles again. "I wouldn't bother, love."

Rope out of the holdall, he advanced on her, and she didn't take his advice. No, she whipped the sock out and opened her mouth wide to scream.

He punched her in the nose a few times, blood spurting, the only sound coming out of her a whimper of pain. Sock back in her gob, he pushed her flat to the floor, loving the fact she'd banged her head. Loving her being in pain.

"You've pissed me *right* off now. I was going to do this when you were dead . . ."

She said something, but it was muffled. He imagined it was: *Do what?*

He dropped the cutters. Looping the rope around her ankles, despite her kicking and flailing and trying to sit up and claw at him, he paused to slap her cheek, and she flopped down again. Wrists secured, he sat on her, holding one of her arms, bringing them both up.

"You know what I said on the phone, yeah?" He picked the cutters up.

She flung her head from side to side, snorting through her nose, snot flying, the dirty bint.

"Well, I always do what I say. I know I said *if* you told the police, but you would have done in the end, wouldn't you."

He snipped off a little finger.

The animalistic noise coming out of her was pretty loud despite the gag, so he cut off all the others quickly, plus the thumbs, blood gushing out. He collected them from where they'd fallen on her chest and put the bloodied things on the sofa, in a row, like the pegs on the table at Georgia's.

Sadly, Nancy was out of it now, unconscious from the pain and shock, he reckoned, so he didn't get to see her reaction when he snipped off her manky toes. They joined the fingers, all twenty stubs lined up together.

Getting off her, he stood and stared at her, this bitch, thinking of how it would feel to kill Mum. Dad.

He found the hammer and brought it down on her skull, the claw end this time, just to mix things up a bit for the police. Give them something to scratch their chins about. He yanked it, and her head rose with it, then dropped away from the claw, grey matter and blood coating it. Claret gushed from the hole, and he gazed at it for ages while it spread on the carpet, a red river.

Mesmerising.

Then he got to work, doing what he'd done to the others, humming *Hush Little Baby* all the while.

Her hoover was crap, though.

CHAPTER EIGHTEEN

The day was another bloody hot one, and Bethany waited outside her house for Mike to join her. He was busy gassing inside with Vinny, who'd had a few hours in bed and would be getting back in it soon.

Her evening with Mike had gone as predicted — lots of shop talk. They'd scrubbed a few suspects off the list: Nancy Forrester, William Bishway, and Liz, Warren, and Georgia Holt.

Mike left the house and got in beside her.

"I just had a thought," she said, waving at Vinny on the doorstep as she drove off.

"What's that then?" Mike plugged his seat belt in.

"What if Harriet Bishway isn't really as frail as she seemed?"

"Oh . . ."

"What if she was so distraught about Chelsea, she killed Jason and Opal? After all, she knew their names, and William was probably in The Fiddler's both nights. Who's to say she didn't just get up and anger gave her the strength to bump them off?"

"Really, though?" He glanced at her, eyebrows high.

"Stranger things have happened. She could have used all that rage she probably feels towards William."

"I suppose so. So what about the bloke buying the printer transfers? There's no way we can discount that. It could be Timothy Bishway."

"Ugh, you always have to be the voice of reason. Ignore me. I was being fanciful."

"I get where you're coming from, but no. It's a bloke."

She parked at the station, and they went inside.

"Oh, Miss Ursula Fringwell, you look absolutely knackered," Bethany said, approaching the front desk.

"I am." She sighed. "What a night. Suspected burglar, a stabbing, ABH, shoplifting from Sainsbury's — a cup with a dog on it, of all things. I tell you, we'll need more holding cells at this rate. Bloody ridiculous."

"Sorry you had a shit time of it. Anything for us?"

"No one's been hoovered out, no."

"Oh, don't," Mike said, walking away and going upstairs.

"Something I said?" Ursula asked, clearly bemused.

"Don't mind him. The poor sod keeps trying to forget seeing that hoover, and I've been a bit of a cow and kept reminding him of it last night."

"You're awful."

"I know." Bethany smiled and waved, then shot up to the incident room.

Kribbs sat with Mike at his desk. Fran and Leona weren't in yet.

"Oh, hello, sir." She moved straight to the coffeemaker, sorting cups while it brewed.

"I just nipped in to say the paperwork for Shoe Zone regarding the boots and Eye Spectacular on the lenses should be with us by the end of play today. They're backlogged, apparently, so it was a good job I applied for it before I went home last night. Going by recent requests, don't hold your breath on it arriving until tomorrow. I think they were being kind in their time estimate — or didn't want me whinging."

"Thanks," she said. "Want a coffee?"

"I wouldn't say no." Kribbs smiled. "How did you get on at the printing shop?"

"We think it's the man. We viewed the CCTV in and out of the shop, plus some from H & M. He bought a large printer pack but also stole a smaller one — stuffed it down his bloody trousers — which we're guessing he used for the eyes on the skull image. He left the shop and disappeared into the crowd."

"Did you get a look at his face?" Kribbs asked.

"No, he had his hood up. Bloody annoying." God, that coffee was taking ages. "I'll get the dongle off to Isabelle, and her lot can work out how tall he is and an average weight."

"What about the boot prints?" Kribbs ran his finger between his shirt collar and his neck. "Full or partials?"

"Toe-end partials, so we don't know what size he takes." She shrugged. "Me and Mike were talking last night and wondered why he'd worn a different pair when killing Opal. Too blood-soaked? If so, where did he put them?"

"If he was sensible, he'd have burnt the buggers. If he wasn't, he'll have dumped them." Kribbs loosened his tie knot.

"You all right, sir?" she asked, concerned that his face was going an unhealthy shade of red.

"Just a bit hot, and I have some things going on that means I lose focus. Health. Nothing to worry about, though. Still, that's neither here nor there. I've got a job to do, just like everyone else. So, I'm off. If you need me, I'll be in my office until lunchtime. Then I'm out for a meal with a few bigwigs."

"Lucky you," she said. "And don't forget your coffee." She quickly poured a cup from what had managed to drip through into the carafe, added Coffeemate and sugar, then handed it over.

"Thanks." He left them to it.

Once the coffee had finally finished brewing, Bethany made another two cups and carried Mike's to him. She leant her backside on his desk and stared at the whiteboards. "Suppose I ought to add what we discovered last night."

She pushed off and went over there, using a marker to update the information. Just as she finished, Fran and Leona walked in with hearty good mornings and got themselves settled at their desks.

"Morning," Bethany said. "Did you have a good evening?"

Fran nodded. "Went to watch a film and ate too much popcorn. Mum babysat, bless her. Much as I love our daughter, I do like spending adult time without her."

"I bet. What about you, Leona?" Bethany asked.

"Ironing. Lots of it. Oh, and cleaning the shower tray. My flat's well grotty, and it keeps getting mouldy. The landlord won't do anything about it. Tight git."

"About time you upped sticks to a better place then, isn't it?" Mike sipped his coffee. "I'll help you on moving day if you like."

"I might have to take you up on that." Leona hung her bag over the back of her chair. "I'll let you know if I ever get my arse in gear and find somewhere else."

"Right." Bethany clapped. "Gossip time over." She told them about their visit to the printing shop.

"He *stole* a pack?" Fran's thin eyebrows joined in the middle. "Cheeky bastard."

"What got me," Bethany said, "was he handed over a twenty, so he could have actually paid for it."

"Ooh, assumption! Just because he had the money, doesn't mean he didn't need it for something else. He might be skint and could only manage to splash out for the big pack." Leona booted up her computer.

Fran chuckled. "He probably is skint, what with buying red contact lenses."

Her dry humour had them all laughing.

"So we're in agreement it's probably this bloke then, yes?" Bethany popped the marker down on the lip at the bottom of the whiteboard.

A general murmur of agreement went round.

"Okay, I'm off to make a couple of calls. Back in a minute." Bethany strode to her office, glanced at the post, and pushed it to one side. It could wait. She dialled Presley after checking he hadn't sent an in-depth email last night.

"Good morning," he said. "I ran late into overtime, hence no update. What a bloody shitshow that PM was. Jason, by the way. I haven't even got around to Opal. She's in the fridge."

Bethany didn't need the visual. "Okay, what have you got on Jason?"

"Wedged up in the chest cavity was a crystal swan and a pink clothes peg."

"What? The swan was stolen from Georgia's house."

"Obviously taken but used straight afterwards. A diamond earring had been poked into the hole in his head."

"That's just bloody sick, that is." She couldn't think why they would have been placed in the body like that. And what was the peg thing all about? "Okay, another crystal was taken — a teardrop. You might find that in Opal."

"I'll certainly look out for it. Like I said before, cause of death is the smack to the head on the hearth spike. Cutting was inflicted after death — stomach and face. I'd say a small spade was used to scrape the remains of the innards out after they were sliced away — there are cut marks all over the cavity where a knife had been used, probably to chop at the liver et cetera. Isabelle has the contact lenses in case they were stupid enough not to wear gloves when applying them. Let's hope a print comes off them."

"Unlikely. Our suspect even wore gloves to buy the printing transfer pack, so it's doubtful he wouldn't have them on while murdering. Right-handed, Isabelle reckons."

"Definitely. Well, I need to get on with Opal's now. I'll let you know if I find a crystal and another earring."

"Or a necklace. That's missing as well."

"Deary me. Bye for now."

She called Isabelle next. "Sorry to bug you so early. Has anything come through?"

"Yes, the digital footprint. Jason had three phones, not two — forgot to tell you I found another one wedged behind a filing cabinet in his home office, which must have been the one he got rid of, pretending he'd lost it. I can only apologise for not keeping you in the loop — so much to do. Okay, so he made many calls to a phone registered to a William Bishway — however, before you get excited, it's clear the messages are from Chelsea, so you might want to check whether Mr Bishway got it for her on contract."

"I can't see that myself," Bethany said. "Timothy Bishway said his father keeps all the money to himself and wouldn't even be likely to part with cash for a gravestone, so I can't see him forking out for a contract, but you never know. I'll look into it."

"Fab. The calls and messages stop a fortnight before she died, so that was when he'd got a new phone — use of his third phone began at the same time. No other use of the second mobile occurred. He had some interesting browsing history . . ."

"Oh God, like what?" Did Bethany want to know? Probably not, but she had to hear it nonetheless. That was the thing about this job. You had to take the sick with the good.

"He liked young girls, put it that way."

"Christ. How young?"

"Teens mainly, although some look about twelve. Disgusting bastard. His Facebook behaviour was clean as a whistle. His laptop, computer, and iPad showed nothing out of the ordinary. He used his personal mobiles, before and after he'd got the new one, to scout online for images, probably because he always had the phones close by and knew no one would touch them — he had fingerprint recognition to open them, but that means nothing to digi forensics, as you know. His work mobile is clean, probably because Georgia had access to it."

It sounded horrible, but Bethany was kind of glad he was dead — and to think she'd told herself he didn't deserve what had happened to him. He'd been a predator just waiting to strike. How many other girls would he have preyed upon if given the chance? She was conflicted, though. From Georgia's description of Chelsea with Jason, it seemed the girl was willing.

"What sort of convos did Chelsea have with Jason?" she asked, needing to clear that query up once and for all.

"She was loved up, and he played to it, the dirty fucker. I'll send it all over to you. We're still waiting on word from the house phone provider. There might be other interesting calls on that. They want paperwork, as usual, so we have to sit tight until they deign to pass on the information. I called Georgia, and they had a paperless bill, and she said she didn't know how to access the online version because Jason dealt with all that sort of thing."

"Wonderful. Another delay." Bethany had some info of her own to share. "You know the crystals and jewellery?"

"Yes."

"The swan crystal was found pushed up into Jason's chest, along with a pink clothes peg — I mean, what the fuck? — and an earring had been put into his head hole."

"Oh, bloody hell. What a sicko."

"I know. Well, I need to get on. Thought I'd leave you with that nice image. Chat soon."

"Have a nice day!"

Bethany smiled and put the phone down. She joined the others in the main room. "Guys, the digital footprint is back for Jason. He scoured the web for images of young girls — I'll get the proper details off Isabelle soon."

"Oh, fuck me," Leona said, frowning. "Bang goes the theory of him not knowing Chelsea was underage."

"Indeed. Seems he probably knew all along." Bethany remembered she hadn't drunk her coffee so poured a fresh one. "So what he'd told Sam King about how he'd met her . . . bullshit or truth? Did he prey on her when he saw her walking past the yard — have we checked if that's on her way home from school? Or was it like King said, and she made a play for Jason? Given her home life, is that why she chose an older man — if it was her doing the choosing — because she desperately wanted a father figure who wasn't a raging tosser?"

"Or King was covering for him and made that scenario up," Mike said. "Maybe he likes the young ones, too. They were best mates. Could have had a shared like for minors."

"Hmm. Maybe we should speak to him again." Bethany shoved a hand through her hair.

"What else was on the report?" Fran asked.

"Isabelle said calls were made to and from a phone registered to William Bishway, but the tone of the written messages and what was said point to it being Chelsea who used it — she seemed like a girl with a crush. I'll ring William now to ask about it. Two secs." She got his number from the board, plugged it into her phone, and walked into the corridor. "Hello, Mr Bishway, this is DI Bethany Smith."

"What do you fucking want?"

Wow. Don't pull your punches then, mate.

"Not a morning person then?" she said, heavy on the sarcasm.

"I'm not a police person. What are you going to accuse me of now? I'm getting ready for work, and you're holding me up."

She'd *string* him up if she had her way.

"I'm not accusing you of anything. I just need to know if you have a contract phone out in your name that Chelsea used."

"Not bleedin' likely. Do you think I'm made of money? No way I'd get a phone for a teenager to use. They run them up, don't they, no thought to whoever's paying the bill."

You've got enough cash to get pissed at the pub.

"So that's a no then," she said.

"Yes, it's a no."

"Would your wife have done it?"

"Bit difficult when she has no dosh to pay for it."

"Thank you." She cut the call without saying goodbye. She didn't need him asking questions about it. Back in the incident room, she said, "He reckons he didn't get the contract, and his wife wouldn't have the funds to pay the bill, so who did?"

"The son? Chelsea herself?" Fran suggested. "Maybe either of them got it in William's name but inputted their own bank details for the direct debit."

"Get on that, will you? How would Chelsea afford it? Did she have a job? Find out what — Hang on." She checked her emails. "Great, the digital info is in from Isabelle. I'll send it to you. Check that number of the phone and find out the billing address if you can. We may need official paperwork for it, but give it a go and see if they'll divulge anything without it. Doubtful, though." She forwarded the email to all three of them. "Done it."

"Okay, thanks." Fran faced her monitor and accessed her Outlook.

"And don't bother with getting back to the pawn shop owners for updates. The swan and an earring were found in Jason. I'm thinking the rest will be in Opal."

"Oh, gross," Leona said.

Bethany's office phone jangled. "Uh-oh." She rushed in there and answered it.

"Hi, it's Alice Jacobs." She sounded out of breath, panicked, which was unusual for the FLO.

"Everything all right?" Bethany's heart pounded. Something wasn't right.

"I'm at Nancy Forrester's — I popped there to see if she was okay."

"And?"

"She's dead."

CHAPTER NINETEEN

"Mum, I need your help," T said, standing at her bedroom doorway, out of breath, his chest hurting from the exertion of running up the stairs and also fear because of what had happened.

Dad was out, so T had no choice but to ask her. He knew she wouldn't give a shit, but he had to try, didn't he? His fingers throbbed from the latest squeezing, and he flexed them gently, wincing at the fresh burst of pain. It was nothing compared to the pain Chelsea was feeling.

Mum sat up in bed, and he hated her so much in that moment. How dare she spend her life there when her children needed her? How dare she stare at him as though she didn't even know who he was? Like she'd forgotten she even had a son.

"What for? I'm tired, T. Sort it yourself." She yawned and scrubbed at her eyes.

How could she be tired when she slept all fucking day and night?

"I think Chelsea's broken her arm," he said through gritted teeth, rage setting off a twitch beside his mouth.

"Take her to the hospital then," she said on an exasperated sigh, as though he was stupid not to have thought of that himself. She flopped back down, drawing the quilt over her head.

Discussion over.

The bitch. What, she was just going to hide like she always did, beneath the covers? Chelsea was in the back garden, crying her eyes out, and her arm had been swelling when he'd rushed up here, and God only knew what it looked like now. Didn't this woman care, even a little bit?

Of course she didn't. Never had.

"They'll ask questions," he said. "I'm seventeen. Won't they wonder why you or Dad aren't with her? What if they ask me stuff?"

"I don't give a toss. Life is too much."

What? Really? He'd known she didn't give a shit, but this was a new low.

He slammed the door, not caring if it set one of her supposed migraines off, and scarpered downstairs, flying out into the garden, his lungs bursting. Mrs Annabelle Pellbody, the youngish brunette widow from next door, hung her ample tits over the low fence, leaning her forearms on it. Christ, he didn't need this, her nosing. She'd ask all sorts of awkward questions.

"She's broken that," she said, nodding towards Chelsea in her all-knowing way. "It needs setting. They'll put it in a cast. Where's your mother? Oh, don't tell me. She's in bed, as usual. Your dad's told me all about that. No wonder he seeks pleasure elsewhere."

There was no need for her to spell it out, gloating. Dad was hardly anyone to brag about. He was no George Clooney. T had long since gathered Dad went round there for—

No, he wouldn't think about it.

He sighed and remembered what Mum had just said. Yes, life was too much, but it didn't stop him from doing what was right, did it? "Yes, she's in bed. She's not interested in helping."

"Now why am I not surprised? She's off her rocker. If she just acted like a normal person, your dad wouldn't get annoyed with her." Mrs Pellbody sniffed. "He's a nice enough man if you just behave yourself."

"Well, we behave ourselves, and it doesn't stop him from hitting me," T snapped, pissed off with her and the crap advice she'd given.

What did she know about living with Dad? What did she know of the terror, the worry, the churning stomach?

He stooped over to help Chelsea stand. "Come on, sis, I'll get you sorted. I'll think of something to say to the nurses."

"You must be doing something wrong if he hits you on the regular, like," Mrs Pellbody said. "A father doesn't whack his kid for no reason."

"I breathe. That's reason enough. You must have heard him shouting through the walls. I'm surprised you want anything to do with a

bully like that." He guided Chelsea towards the back door, and her whimpers tore at his heart. Pitiful, they were.

"I'll take her if you want," Mrs Pellbody said. "To the hospital. Got a car, haven't I. It'll be quicker. So long as you say you fell in my back garden, Chels, which is why I've taken you to A and E, everything should work out."

Maybe this wouldn't end up so bad after all. There'd be no need to go into details of why Mum hadn't got her arse out of bed to tend to her child's needs. Why Dad hadn't answered his phone when T had rung him and come home to collect Chelsea. T reckoned Mrs Pellbody wasn't so bad either, not if she was willing to help them like this.

"Besides, it'll put me even more in your dad's good books, won't it."

Whatever her reasons, T didn't care. "Is that okay with you, Chelsea?"

She nodded, her face so white he worried she'd faint.

"It hurts so much."

He brushed her tears away with his thumb. "I know. Go with Mrs Pellbody, all right? Say what she tells you to."

Chelsea nodded again, and he took her through the house to meet their neighbour out the front.

"I saw you fall and land funny," Mrs Pellbody said, trotting down her path on high heels, "so there's no worries about any nefarious behaviour."

Nefarious? Had she swallowed a bloody dictionary or what?

"In the car with you," she said.

T stood there until she'd driven out of sight, for ages and ages, then Dad's car replaced it on the kerb outside the house, the wheel arches going rusty, scabs on an otherwise decent vehicle.

"What the fuck are you doing just standing there?" he said as he got out. "You look like a right mong."

Dad had no idea you weren't meant to use words like that anymore. Come to think of it, the arsehole wouldn't care.

T glared at him. "Chelsea broke her arm. Your girlfriend took her to hospital."

"Good. Saves me the job."

No denial about the girlfriend then.

Dad strolled towards him. "Now get inside and sort my dinner out. Some of us have been working all day and need a full belly."

"Some of us have been to college all day and need to revise for exams," T shot back.

"No, what you need is to watch your mouth, you arrogant little tosser." Dad squared up to him on the path, his chest puffed up, arms in that bugging position at his sides.

"Going to hit me in front of the neighbours, are you?" T asked.

Dad stomped to the house.

"Didn't think so. Twazzock."

Dad didn't stop walking. Didn't look back. How the tide had turned. Gone were the days where T had to keep his mouth shut, fearing he'd get hurt. Now, he was just biding his time until Chelsea was sixteen, then he'd take her far away from this pair of bastards.

He refused to go in and start the dinner. Mum and Dad could go and fuck themselves, just like him and Chelsea had to. Instead, he walked to the river, to the point close to the hospital car park so he could watch for Chelsea and Mrs Pellbody leaving. He'd run over and meet them when they came out, bag a lift home.

Swans coasted on the surface, staring at him as though they had a mind to bite him if he went too close, their beady black eyes staring and sinister. A tear fell down his cheek, and he didn't bother wiping it away.

Sometimes, even strong lads needed to cry.

A woman walked by in a sparkling diamond necklace and matching earrings, giving him a look of pity. T reckoned they'd cost her a fortune, and he wondered about life and how unfair it was that some people were rich while others drowned in poverty. The tutors at college said life was what you made it, and if you wanted nice things, you'd work hard in order to get them, but what about those people born with a silver spoon in their mouths? Where did their work come into it? What about those born without a pot to piss in, who, no matter how many degrees they had, they still couldn't get a decent job? And what about him and Chelsea, living a life where the only love they got was from each other?

Swans, tears, and jewels. They'd forever remind him of the fact that today, more than any other, he'd discovered that his parents truly didn't care. One had remained in bed despite her child needing her, and the other had been glad someone else was taking responsibility.

T would never do that to Chelsea. He'd look after her until his dying day.

CHAPTER TWENTY

Bethany and Mike stood in Nancy's living room, the air thick with the stench of not only her cigarettes but blood, so much blood. This was the third sight of the same method of murder, someone who stuck to the tried and tested — except for her fingers and toes perched in a line of the sofa as though they'd got up and positioned themselves there. It was damn creepy.

"Christ Almighty," Mike said, rubbing his lips with his fingers.

"Bit of an escalation in terms of the fingers and toes," Isabelle said.

Bethany stared at the mess left on the hands and feet, growing queasy.

"And see the head wound there?" Isabelle pointed — Jesus, as if any of them needed help in where to look. "Hammer again, I'm betting you, but the claw side this time."

Bethany retched.

"The hole is different, see?" Isabelle seemed intent on getting them to have a closer gander — or pushing Bethany into being sick.

This is just a tad too much. How does Tracy Collier do this all the time? How does she cope?

Bethany could compartmentalise once she got home, but at work, when it was in her face all day, she had to deal with it. Preferably without throwing up.

Isabelle hunkered down. "I think some brain came free but can't see it on or around her."

"Oh, bloody hell." Bethany turned away for a moment to compose herself.

"The stomach has been hoovered again," Mike said. "Her vacuum is over there. It's got another of those see-through dirt catchers, except it isn't just dirt in there. It's the hoover all over again."

Bethany checked the top right-hand corner of the room and, sure enough, a value-brand hoover stood with a belly full of innards scrapings. Despite her nauseated state, she walked over there and peered at the transparent section to see if anything else was visible. A layer of dust at the bottom, and red gunk above it. On top, partially submerged, pieces of white card about a centimetre square.

"It's looks like it has another contact lens box in it," she said. "It's such a pisser that we won't hear back from Eye Spectacular until tomorrow." She explained the lateness of the paperwork. "By the time we get it, the company might be shut for phone calls, so we'll have to wait until the morning. It frustrates the shit out of me that they have the information we need sitting on their computers, and there's nothing we can do about it. The killer's name is there, and he could do this again before we have a chance to stop him." She looked at Mike for his brand of calming her panic.

"Don't worry so much. Seems this person prefers killing at night, so we have time." He shoved his hands into his pockets, showing her: *If I'm not bothered, why should you be?*

She returned her focus to Nancy Forrester. The skinned face. Red contacts. The skull image. Gross as it was, she moved to stand beside her to see if she spotted a peg or the teardrop crystal in her chest, but all that met her scrutiny was a mass of burgundy matter.

Isabelle did the walk-through around the house with them next. The bathroom had been used, but only a tiny speck of blood sat on the silver ring of the plughole, visible only through the SOCO's magnifying lens, so their killer had got better at cleaning up after himself.

With no time to wait for Presley and his opinion on time of death, Bethany and Mike left and sat in the car.

She rang Leona. "Where does William Bishway work?"

"Two seconds."

She slid the key in the ignition and started the engine. Windows open — the sun was fierce again; when the hell would it rain? — she tapped the fingers of her free hand on the steering wheel, irritating herself with the noise it made.

"Hammond's," Leona said. "The carpet and tile shop-slash-warehouse."

"Thanks. We're nipping there because I want to ask him a few questions about his son. I'll tell you the outcome when we get back — unless it's something I need you to look into. We've just been in to see Nancy Forrester. Same as the others, except she had her fingers and toes cut off, and the claw end of a hammer was used on her head."

"Ouch."

"I know. Doesn't bear thinking about, does it. Catch you soon."

She popped her phone in the drink holder between the seats and drove away.

"What are you thinking of asking William?" Mike propped his elbow on the window ledge, the breeze flapping his shirt sleeve.

"Whether Timothy got any deliveries before he moved out."

"Good thinking."

They arrived at Hammond's, and Bethany introduced them to the rather uptight receptionist behind a glass desk — mid-forties, red hair, the colour out of a bottle, a savage shade of cerise on her lips. A door to the left had SHOWROOM on it, and they were told to go through, and Mr Dagley, the manager, would meet them.

A vast space filled with rolls of carpet on one side, half-way down another, then a tile section at the bottom, had Bethany taking a moment to get her bearings. People at the end appeared small it was that far away, and she had a few seconds of disorientation. A grey-haired man in a dark suit made his way towards them but stopped momentarily to talk to an elderly customer. He pointed to a stack of rugs then continued walking. Bethany and Mike strode ahead to meet him.

"DI Bethany Smith and DS Mike Wilkins," she said, brandishing her ID. "We need to speak to an employee, William Bishway, about his son. Where is he?" She glanced about.

"He's not in today, I'm afraid."

"Oh. He said he was getting ready for work earlier this morning when I rang him." She couldn't care less if she got him in the shit.

"He called in sick, sorry."

Bloody hell. "Okay, thanks."

They left, and in the car, heading towards the Bishway's house, she said, "Is it him, do you reckon? William?"

"I can't see it. He's too broad and not quite tall enough to be the bloke on the printer shop CCTV."

"What about both of them then — father and son?" She indicated right and took the turn. "What if they've both made up a bullshit story where they're pretending they dislike each other to throw us off?"

Mike shrugged. "Could be. It's frustrating the hell out of me, I know that much. Three murders, three nights. Do we suppose Nancy was killed because she's related to Opal? I mean, the poor sod has nothing to do with Chelsea, other than being Opal's mother."

"Who knows when it comes to the mind of a deranged person?" She parked up the road from the Bishway's. "Do you know what? I'm going to ring that Tracy Collier woman."

"What?"

"Maybe she'll see something we don't if I tell her what's going on." She got her phone out and rang the station where Tracy Collier worked. She was put through to her office, and, with her stomach rolling, she said, "Sorry to bother you. I'm DI Bethany Smith from Shadwell, and I wondered if I could bend your ear."

"Shadwell. Lovely . . ." Tracy said. "I heard you've got a big job on your hands there. Good luck with it, but if you think I'm coming to the city if I don't have to, you've got another think coming. That place isn't somewhere I ever want to be if I can avoid it."

Christ, what a salty tart.

"Believe me, I don't *want* you here," she snapped back, bristling, realising now why people had said Collier was a bitch. "I just want to run this by you to see if we've missed something that's glaringly obvious."

"I don't really have time. I have my own murder to deal with."

"Okay, not to worry. Don't blame me if my boss gets me to call you again, though. You're the head of serious crimes and also have to come to my patch if things get out of hand here — whether either of us like it or not."

A massive sigh chuntered down the line. "I'm aware of that. Look, give me what you've got. Verbally. I don't want the files. Like I said, limited time. I can't be arsed with reading it all. The condensed version — don't go around the bloody houses."

Wow. She's . . . acerbic.

Nervous at having to say it all in one go, and because of the woman's arsey, abrupt manner, Bethany swallowed then plunged in. At the end of it all, which had taken her twenty minutes, with her conscious of wasting the woman's precious seconds, she said, "What do you think?"

"Right, first off, if you suspect the son, which is where your mind is at whether you realise it or not, his broken fingers as a kid bother me."

"What have they got to do with anything?"

"Think outside the box. Did you get a chance to look at them at all?"

Bethany thought back to when she'd seen Timothy. He'd held his hand up to show her his fingers. "Yes, they're all crooked."

"Okay, and what about his nails? You said the printer shop bloke noticed they were weird."

"No, I didn't see those. He had his palm outwards."

"That's a bit of a bummer. So have you looked at the crime scene photos?"

"Not really had the time to look at them — Isabelle, our lead SOCO, is still studying them. We've had three murders back to back, so sitting down to view photos hasn't been a priority."

"So go and look at them. Somewhere there might be a crooked-finger handprint."

"Thank you so much." *Fuck it.* Bethany felt incompetent. Why hadn't she thought of that? Harriet had mentioned the finger squeezing, Timothy had mentioned them being broken, and now Collier was going to think she was a bloody prat for not 'thinking outside the box' — a box she hadn't realised she was trapped in until now.

The new perspective could end up solving this case.

Tracy sighed again. "Listen, if you're anything like me, you'll be kicking yourself now, but I'll let you in on a secret. I'm not a total bitch, really, I just give off that air, but I fuck up. Often. I forget things — forget to check them. My mind gets too full of everything. It's easy for me to see what you've missed because I'm on the outside, so instead of pissing and moaning about missing it, blaming yourself, move on and catch the bastard. Now, I'm off. You're welcome."

The line went dead.

"Bloody Nora!" Bethany stared at her phone. "That woman is seriously — and I mean *seriously* — scary."

"What did she say?"

"She's so . . .forthright." She went on to fill him in.

Mike laughed. "She's right, though." He tapped his forehead. "The mind *does* get too full. We can't possibly remember everything, not when there's so much going on."

"But it's standard to check the images properly, and I didn't."

"I know, but like you said, we've been busy, and Isabelle didn't tell you the handprints had wonky fingers, so it's not all on you. And it might not even be that — the dodgy fingers, I mean. But we've got a chance to fix it now."

She rang Isabelle. "Hi. Are there any handprints in the crime scene photos?"

"Not full ones, no."

"Are there any fingers?"

"Only the tips. Why?"

"There's been a question brought up about wonky fingers."

"Okay . . ."

"It doesn't matter. If you haven't spotted any, this call is moot. I have to go. Thanks."

She pocketed her phone.

"Get the car going and drive to the RSPCA centre," Mike said. "We'll surprise him at work. Have a good look at his nails."

"Right. Yes. Thank you for being the voice of reason. Again. I hate to say this, but I'm glad I rang Tracy, even if she turns out to be right, because it means, if the bastard has another kill planned, we'll stop him before he has the chance."

She sped off. They arrived in no time and spoke to the same woman they'd seen before. Dogs barked in the background, faint, as though the kennel section was far away, some vocalisations low and gruff, some high yips and yaps.

"Oh, he's not in yet," she said, scratching the end of her nose. It was red, as if she suffered from hay fever. "He does shifts. Today he's on . . . Actually, let me just check." She scooted back on her wheeled desk chair and looked at a small whiteboard on the wall. "Oh. He's not in until tomorrow now."

"Cheers." Bethany smiled.

They left.

"What's his address?" she asked Mike once they were on their way again.

He pulled out his notebook. "Seventeen Birchwood Rise."

"That's pretty close to here."

It took five minutes to get there. Bethany parked outside, and at the door, she knocked — hard. A minute or so passed after someone shouted, "Hang on!" Then a man answered, black hair wet and tousled, a powder-blue towel around his waist, water droplets clinging to the sparse hairs on his chest.

She explained who they were. "Is Timothy in?"

"No idea. I've not long got home. I stayed at my bird's house last night, see. Just had a shower, didn't hear him about."

"Can you go and check, please?"

"Come in. You can do it. First door at the top of the stairs after the bathroom. If he's dodgy, I don't want anything to do with it."

"Dodgy?"

"Well, you're here, aren't you? Plus, he's weird."

Her heart hammered. "In what way?"

"I don't know. Just . . . odd."

They stepped inside.

"I'll just check the downstairs first," Mike said and disappeared into the living room.

Bethany turned to the man. She couldn't remember what Timothy had said his housemates' names were. "And you are?"

"Ben Chadwell." He closed the front door, seemingly at ease being half naked in front of strangers.

She asked the next question in case Timothy had been lying. "Do you share the house with anyone else other than Timothy?"

"Yes, Cassandra."

Cassandra? That rings a bell. "Cassandra what?"

"Volten. She'll be at work, though."

"Where's that?"

"In an office during the day, dunno where, and The Fiddler's at night."

Bethany filed that info away. It had to be the same Cassandra the manager at the pub had mentioned. If she could speak to her, they'd be able to find out whether he was also there on the night of Jason's murder. "What about you?"

"I'm a boiler engineer. Got the day off — self-employed."

Mike went into the kitchen and came back out again. "I'll look in all the rooms upstairs if that's still okay?" He cocked his head at Ben.

"Be my guest." Ben held his hand out, gesturing to the stairs. "What's Timothy done?"

"I can't discuss that," Bethany said. "You could help by answering questions, though. You said you were at your girlfriend's house last night. What about the two nights previous?"

"Out on the lash." He scratched his head. "I went into the city on a pub crawl both evenings — that was with my mates — then went clubbing. Hence the day off. I worked with hangovers the past two days. Knackered now."

"What about Cassandra?"

"She'll have been at work. She's saving for a deposit to buy her own place so takes all the hours she can get. She'll do herself some damage keep pushing herself so hard."

"So neither of you were home for the last three nights." She didn't expect an answer. No one would have seen Timothy coming and going, the house being empty. Maybe the neighbours would have spotted something. She'd get the uniforms down here to ask some questions. Even if it wasn't Timothy they were after, it wouldn't hurt.

Mike came back down. "No one."

Bethany turned to Ben. "Mr Chadwell, if Timothy comes back, could you give me a ring without him knowing, please?" She handed him her card.

"Yep. Do I need to be worried?"

She couldn't tell him a thing so just said, "Sleep with one eye open — or go and stay with your 'bird' for a few nights."

"Fucking hell . . . Um, I have a key to her place. I'll go there in a sec."

"Good. Give it about three days, all right? If you can get hold of Cassandra and advise her to do the same."

"She can come with me. My girlfriend's her mate."

"Lovely. Well, thanks for your time. Sorry to have bothered or worried you."

In the car again, she rang the uniforms, Glen Underby and Nicola Eccles, to come down and do door-to-door, then they headed to the Bishway's.

"Let's see if he's gone round to see Mummy," Bethany said.

On the doorstep, she rang the bell, but no one came to the door. Music blasted out from inside, and someone was singing *Total Eclipse of the Heart* a bit too enthusiastically.

Mike stepped off the path and peered through the nets hanging at the living room window. "Um, you might want to come here, Beth."

She stood beside him, bent over, and squinted, seeing into the room via a pattern hole in the fabric.

Harriet Bishway stood with a microphone, belting out the lyrics, the words coming up on the TV. She swayed from side to side, seeming full of energy and life, a stark contrast to the hunched-up figure Bethany had seen in the bed.

Bethany stood upright and gaped at Mike. "What the *bloody hell?*"

CHAPTER TWENTY-ONE

Georgia left the hotel and rushed along the street. She needed a few bits and bobs from Boots, and her doctor had given her some tablets this morning to help cope with not being able to sleep. Liz had gone with her to the surgery, not wanting Georgia to be alone.

I'll get my prescription filled while I'm at it.

Liz and Warren had offered to come with her to the shops, 'to keep you safe', but to be honest, she was sick of their company. Much as she loved them, she needed some space, a moment or twenty to gather her raging thoughts. They swung from her being angry as eff with Jason for what he'd been like staring at young blonde women, and sad that she was alone now. It was a roller coaster of a ride, this grief thing, and she'd feel better if she could just *be* for a while. Besides, it was daylight. She'd be fine.

Three quarters of the way to the row of nearby shops, she wondered if she *would* be fine after all. She got the uneasy feeling that someone was watching her, so she hurried even faster, glancing over her shoulder every so often, amazed to see that no one followed. So why did she feel as though they did?

Her heartrate skittered.

"Stupid cow," she muttered, reaching the shops at last and pushing inside Boots, relieved to smell the familiar scent this shop had no matter which one you went into. Perfume, from the counter to the left, most likely.

She collected her prescription then grabbed a basket. Dry shampoo — she had no desire to mess about with washing her hair at the moment. Deodorant — she'd forgotten to pack some and had to keep borrowing Liz's, which meant more interaction than she wanted. A pack of multivitamins — in the hopes it would give her some energy. She hadn't been to work since Jason had died, and in four days, she'd be returning.

I need to sort myself out before then. Can't be dealing with patients when I'm so tired.

She left the shop and looked left then right, scanning the area for anyone who appeared even remotely threatening. God, this was stupid, but her gut was screaming that something was wrong. Everyone seemed normal, though, so she headed back towards the hotel.

Her phone rang, and she fumbled with the zip on her bag, praying she'd get to her mobile before the caller hung up. Thankfully, she managed it and, glancing at the screen, noticed the number wasn't a name in her contact list but had been withheld.

"Hello?" she said, thinking it might be Bethany Smith, hoping the policewoman had found the killer and Georgia wouldn't have to worry anymore.

"Good day to you. I'm calling from Bishway Solutions, and I'd like to offer you a free trial for justice served—"

She severed the connection. "Bloody cold callers."

It rang again.

"Good day to you. I'm calling from Bishway Solutions—"

"Oh, go away."

End call.

A third ring.

"Good day to you. I'm calling from Bishway Solutions, and if you don't fucking listen to me, I'll kill you quicker than I intended."

Oh God, Oh God, Oh God . . .

Her heart all but rattled, and she gulped a breath into her tight lungs. Quicker than he intended? What? "Who are you?" It came out ragged, proving how scared she was, and she hated that he'd know that he'd freaked her the hell out.

"Wouldn't you like to know." He sounded like he was in two places at once — in the phone and somewhere close by.

Her legs threatened to give way, and she gazed around, frantic, convinced he was near her and she just couldn't see him. "Please, whatever Jason did to upset you, it's nothing to do with me." She ducked into an alley, head bent, wanting to gather herself for a moment in private, away from the keen gaze of anyone, people walking towards the shops or away from them. The Ringer Hotel was only a few metres along the road now, but if she—

Georgina smacked straight into someone.

Someone holding a phone to his ear.

Someone who smiled at her, but it was sinister. Chilling.

Someone who said, "Good day. You've just bumped into the CEO of Bishway Solutions."

* * *

T punched her in the face, and she went down like a sack of shit, a startled half-screech coming out of her bleeding mouth, her phone going airborne then crashing to the ground.

"Shut your gob, understand?" he snarled, anger fizzing inside.

She looked up at him, her eyes wide, fearful — and she needed to fear him. He'd planned to bump her off tonight, but now she'd seen him, and he'd introduced himself, there was no going back. He hadn't expected her to come down the alley, and that had just messed with his plans.

"What do you want from me?" she said, the words shaky, blood dripping down her chin from her split lip.

"What I want is for you to shut your gob, like I just said. Get the fuck up."

He dragged her to standing and marched her down the alley, coming out on a disused bit of wasteland, the grass yellow and dried from the lack of rain, broken bricks here and there, and the river.

The deepest part of the river.

It flowed behind The Ringer, and he'd have to be careful. Anyone might be looking out, see him, and call the police.

"Look what you've made me do," he snapped at her. "Stupid cow."

"I didn't make you do anything," she whimpered, stumbling along.

"You don't follow directions well, do you? I told you to keep your trap shut. So do as I said."

His hoodie covered the majority of his face, so he wasn't that bothered about people being able to identify him, it was the getting caught that was the problem.

Why hadn't he just walked past her when she'd turned into the alley and pretended he was on the phone to someone else? Why had he blurted out he was her caller?

Thick bastard.

"Get the hell over there," he said, shoving her closer to the river's edge.

She obeyed, staying quiet, and he wondered why she didn't scream. Someone from out in the street would come rushing to help her if she did. Was she stupid or what? Didn't she have the survival instinct in her? He decided he didn't care enough to find out.

He stooped.

Swiped up a brick.

And smashed her head in with it.

* * *

Bethany stared at Harriet in the Bishway's living room. "You suddenly got some energy."

Harriet blushed, keeping busy by putting the karaoke machine away behind a chair. "It's none of your business what I do. If I want to sing every day when no one's home, then I'll bloody well sing."

Bethany thought of Timothy and Chelsea, of the life they'd supposedly lived with this curiously odd woman and her bully of a husband. "Have you always sung every day?"

"So what if I have? No crime in it, is there?" Her voice was full of belligerence.

"Not in the lawful sense, no, but the moral sense? Yes. Staying in bed all day pretending to be ill so you presumably don't have to deal with your children is disgusting. Making out to people like me that you're so broken you can't leave your bed is deceitful and mean."

"Oh, fuck off. You have no idea why I do it. No clue what it's like living with William."

The change in the woman was staggering. She'd gone from meek and mild to bolshy and loud. Would she have been this way if Bethany and Mike hadn't caught her having a party for one? Or would she have played her usual part, pretending she was some insipid individual who wouldn't say boo to a goose?

"I just have a question for you, then I'll leave you to get on with your crap Bonnie Tyler impression." Bethany had the urge to punch this bitch in the face. The sympathy had dried up. "Before Timothy moved out, did he get any parcels delivered?"

"Yes, why? What's that got to do with you?"

"I'm a detective on a double murder enquiry, *that's* what it has to do with me. You're a citizen who may have information that will help in that enquiry, and it's in your best interests to give it to me. How big were they?"

"Whatever it was came in a white padded envelope. One of the bigger ones. Now get out. I need to have a bath before I get back in bed. William will be home soon."

"You might want to forego the bath. He isn't at work today and could come home any second and catch you."

"Shit!"

Bethany shook her head. "I don't know how you can live with yourself. I realise your husband hits you but—"

Harriet laughed, a crazy, she's-lost-the-plot laugh. "What?"

"The bruises on your face. Timothy said his father hit you." Bethany frowned.

"It's what I wanted people to believe. I hit myself. With doors. Walls. My fist." She hissed that last word, stepping forward, and she looked feral, totally unhinged.

"Why would you do that?" Bethany couldn't believe this.

"Is my answer needed for your investigation?" Harriet cocked her head. "Didn't think so. Now piss off."

Bethany walked out. The woman was out of her mind, and Bethany didn't want to be on the receiving end of her madness. They got in the car, and Mike stared across at her.

"What. Was. That?" he said.

"I have no idea. She's spent her marriage purposely hurting herself and making out she's ill? Why?"

"She's broken — long before Chelsea died."

"I agree, and she needs help. We'll get it for her — if she'll take it — but first, we need to get back to the station and check those photos, see if Isabelle missed anything—" Her phone interrupted. She jabbed the screen to accept. "Yep? What's up, Rob?"

"Call came in," he said. "Someone witnessed a man beating a woman to death behind The Ringer, then he dumped her in the river."

"What?" she screeched.

"Uniform are on scene — they got there too late to catch the bloke, though. Apparently, the body got caught on a low-hanging tree branch, one that dips into the water."

"Bloody hell. We'll go there now."

"There's more," Rob said.

"What is it?"

"Georgia Holt is missing."

* * *

After her body had hit the water with an almighty splash, T had raced to where he'd parked his van and sped off, covered in blood, shaking, asking himself again what the fuck he'd been playing at. This wasn't how it was supposed to go. He had a plan, and he'd gone off course. How could he get inside his home without being clocked?

"Damn it," he said, whacking the steering wheel, accidentally hitting the horn and earning himself a few startled glances from people walking the streets. "That's it, bring attention to yourself, you dickwad."

He reached home and cut the engine on the driveway, looking all around to check for any neighbours. Seeing no one, he got his keys ready so there would be no delay, then rushed indoors, legging it upstairs and into the bathroom in case Ben or Cassandra were home.

He got in the shower fully clothed so the blood washed off easier, then undressed and lathered his body and hair. The pink water swirling down the plughole annoyed him — that blood should be in the bath at The Ringer, in Georgia's room. He rinsed himself then shut the water off and wrung his clothing, so tight they resembled liquorice sticks. His white T-shirt still had stains on it, but he couldn't sort it out now. Out of the tub, he took the liner from the bin and shoved his clothes inside. A pink towel hung on the back of the door hook — not his — but he didn't think Cassandra would mind if he used it. Dried, he wrapped it around his waist, made sure no blood remained anywhere, then took the bag into his bedroom. He tied it, stashed it under the bed, got dressed, and checked all the upstairs rooms.

No one.

He went to the living room and kitchen, but his housemates weren't there either. Relaxing a bit, he thought again about what had happened, how he'd royally screwed things up.

"What's done is done," he said, trying to convince himself everything would be okay. "But it won't. It'll never be okay with those two fuckers still living."

He used the old-fashioned green phone and dialled.

She picked up. "Yes?" Her voice, so groggy, like it always was.

He prepared himself to put on a Scottish accent so she wouldn't recognise his voice. "Good day to you, Harriet. I'm calling from Bishway Solutions, and I'd like to offer you a free trial for justice served—"

"What?" She seemed more alive that time. Alert. Confused.

"I'm coming for you," he said, all growly and menacing. "And him."

"Who is this?"

Oh, her voice had changed completely, to something he imagined she'd sound like if she wasn't so 'depressed'. He frowned, unable to compute it.

"Who do you think it is?" he asked.

"William?"

Why would she think it was Dad? He wasn't from bloody Scotland.

"No, not William. Try again."

"I don't know, do I, you fucking dickhead!" That was loud, confident, and so unlike her. "Piss off and ring someone else."

He slammed the receiver down and threw himself out of the house and into the van. Driving fast, he made it to his childhood home in minutes, using his old key to get inside. He raced upstairs, and Mum was in the bed, on her side in her usual pathetic position. She lifted her head as though too tired to do so, but he knew better. She'd just spoken to him full of life on the phone.

"Speak to me," he said, moving to the side of the bed so he could look down at her.

"Oh, Timothy, it's you . . ." That voice belonged to an old, decrepit lady, not the voice he'd listened to when he'd called her.

It didn't make sense.

"I've come to tell you that I hate you," he said, goading her to talk in that other way again. "That you're a bitch for what you put me and Chelsea through."

"Like I care," she said. "Don't be mean."

"Mean? *This* is mean." He bent over her, grabbed Dad's pillow, and shoved it on her face.

Climbing on top of her, he pressed it down, and she struggled with more energy than she should have had if her so-called, constant lethargic state was anything to go by. Her muffled cries spurred him on, and he pushed harder, shutting his eyes and recalling his childhood, all the times she hadn't given a toss about him and Chelsea.

She stopped moving after a few minutes, and he waited, arms aching from the constant pressure, still seeing images flickering through his mind, reliving them, hating her with every part of him — his cells, his muscles, his bones. Cheeks streaked with tears, he opened his eyes and removed the pillow. Her face . . . he couldn't look at it. If he did, he'd want to skin the bloody thing, and he didn't have his tools with him. They were in the van, and he wasn't going to go out there to get them. He got off her and punched her instead, then went downstairs to wait.

It didn't take long before Mrs Pellbody's front door slammed shut and this one opened. T waited in the living room doorway with Dad's baseball bat in hand, the one he kept handy for intruders, not that he'd had to use it.

Well, T was going to use it now.

He waited for Dad to walk past, going into the kitchen, then chased after him, bringing the bat down on the back of his head. And he kept smacking it, big swings, short swings, all the rage coming out of him at last.

'Christ, I need you two like I need a hole in the head.'

And T had kept to his promise, putting a hole in Dad's.

He hit and hit and hit until the head wasn't a head anymore. It was mush. Blood everywhere.

Spent and calm now, he had a shower, slung on some of his old clothes he'd left there before moving out, then strolled from that house for good, got his bag from the back of the van, and strode up Mrs Pellbody's path.

He couldn't risk her trying to get hold of Dad now, could he, and finding out what he'd done.

CHAPTER TWENTY-TWO

The sun beat down on the back of Bethany's neck, hot and relentless, and her skin itched from the severity. She stared at Georgia, who had been pulled from the river in an attempt to save her life, but it was so clear she wasn't coming back from the battering. The top of her head might as well not exist it had been hit so many times, her face skinned in a very different way to the other victims, scraped off by the brick lying a few feet away — and there was no question in her mind that this was the same killer. She couldn't claim coincidence. This woman had been involved in the terrible game Jason had played, and she was a part of it whether she'd wanted to be or not. The killer had targeted her regardless of whether she'd been an innocent in this. She hadn't been safe at all, no matter that she'd done nothing to deserve this.

Nothing we know of anyway.

That thought didn't sit well, but it was something to consider. Perhaps things would come out along the way in the investigation — maybe she'd done something they weren't aware of yet.

It firmly put paid to the idea Georgia might be the killer — or had got someone to do it for her. Then again, the killer might have come after her. She might not have settled their bill. It was something to ponder.

Presley stood beside the body on the opposite side to Bethany, and he shook his head. "I can't see me finding anything inside her, what with her torso still intact, but that's not to say something isn't inside that mess of what used to be her head. I'll check it when I do the PM." He rubbed his chin with his sleeve. "Oh, by the way, a pink peg, the teardrop crystal, and another earring was found in Opal Forrester. The earring matches the one inside Jason."

"I wonder what the significance is?" she said.

"If any." Mike wiped the sweat off his forehead with the shirt material over his upper arm. "Maybe they just thought it would get our heads messed up or we'd waste time following that line of investigation."

"Whatever, it's sick." She sighed. "Well, we know the time of death on this one, Presley, so we don't need to bother you with that."

He crouched. "Seeing as the photos have been taken . . ." He pulled down her blood-spattered top by her throat.

Bethany gasped. "That's her sodding necklace, the one she said was stolen."

"It might well have been," Mike said, "and the killer gave it back."

She frowned. "This is doing my nut in."

"Which might be the point." Mike smiled.

Isabelle, who had been talking to SOCOs over at the kill site, strolled their way, only her eyes visible beneath the white suit hood and above her face mask. She stood beside Bethany. "What a nightmare, eh?"

"I know." Bethany grimaced. "This needs to end. There's been too much bloodshed, and we're meant to be finding Timothy Bishway. This happened, so it's been put on hold. We're now going to have to go back to his house, see if he's there, then fit in talking to the witness in the hotel — and go to see Liz and Warren Holt." Just the idea of cramming all that in had her head spinning.

"We'd better get a move on then," Mike said.

They walked to the car, stripped off their protective clothing, and Bethany put it in a bag on the back seat. She drove them to Timothy's new home, but no one was in. She prayed Ben and Cassandra would stay away for a few days. If Timothy was the killer, those two didn't need to be caught up in this.

Back in the car, she took them to The Ringer and got the room number from the receptionist of the man who'd seen the murder. Bethany and Mike used the stairs, seeing as the witness was only on the first level, and she knocked on room two.

The door swung open, and a uniform, Nicola Eccles, stood there. "He's in the loo throwing up." She pointed to the door beside her. Lowering her voice, she said, "His name's Andrew Lakes."

They stepped in and waited in the living room area for the man to emerge. He stumbled in, his face still wet from where he'd presumably splashed it with cold water. The scent of toothpaste came off him.

"Mr Lakes, I'm DI Bethany Smith, and this is DS Mike Wilkins. I'm so sorry to have to ask questions that Nicola already has, but needs must. Have a seat." She gestured to the sofa.

He sat, appearing shaky and off kilter.

"Mr Lakes, can you tell me from the beginning what happened?"

He nodded. "I was having a sneaky cigarette out of the window." He blushed. "I know, I know, it's not allowed. I was leaning right out to stop too much smoke coming back in. From where I was, you can see the exit of an alleyway that leads onto the scrubland."

Bethany went over there, opened the window, and leant out. The alley was about five hundred metres away. SOCO appeared tiny from here, their white suits glaring in the sunshine, the officers milling about beside the river.

"What happened then?" She closed the window.

"A man dragged a woman over to a patch of grass where there are a few piles of rubble, by the river. He just started whacking her in the head with what I assumed was a brick, then when she was on the ground, he was messing about near her neck. I thought he was strangling her at first. After that, he picked her up, threw her in the bloody water, then ran away."

"Which way did he run?"

"Back down the alley."

Fantastic. He could be caught on CCTV.

"I've rung Rob about it, and he's passing it on to Fran and Leona," Nicola said.

"Thank you." Bethany smiled at her. The quicker CCTV was accessed, the better.

She chatted to him a bit more, then, with nothing much else to say, they left and headed for Liz Holt's room, which faced the front of the hotel and thankfully not the back where SOCOs were doing their thing in plain sight. She didn't need them looking out and seeing the tent, which had probably been erected by now.

Bethany knocked on the door, and an anxious-looking Warren opened it.

"Come in," he said. "I've been sitting with Mum. We're so worried. Georgia's not answering her phone."

Shit. He thought they were there about her going missing.

Bethany and Mike stepped inside. Liz sat on the bed, and Warren took a seat in the living area.

"Do you know what time Georgia went out?" Bethany asked.

"We didn't even know she'd *gone* out again." Warren shook his head. "She went to the doctor's with Mum this morning. Why would she go out a second time without one of us?"

"Maybe she went to the shops," Liz said, wringing her hands. "She had a prescription to fill."

Bethany took a deep breath. "I'm sorry to inform you of this, but Georgia was murdered."

"What?" Warren jumped up.

Liz howled and flopped backwards on the bed. Warren went to her, kneeling beside it and holding her hands. Bethany and Mike waited until the noise had died down and Liz pulled herself upright.

"How can this be happening?" Liz said, staring at them with puffy eyes.

"We think it has something to do with Jason and his affair," Bethany said. "Do you want to hear the details? Though I'm not sure you'll be able to deal with it at the moment."

"Tell us." Liz nodded. "Just give it all to us. I'd rather know now than find out about it on the bloody news."

Bethany jumped in with both feet. "Jason was seeing a young girl who unfortunately got pregnant. She was fifteen."

Liz groaned, her eyes closing momentarily, and Warren swore.

Bethany continued. "She went for a termination and, due to an unknown heart problem, died during the operation. We feel the person who killed Jason has an axe to grind."

"I should bloody think so if she's fifteen!" Warren paced, his face going red. "If I was her dad, I'd skin him alive." His choice of words seemed to hit him, and he closed his eyes for a second or two. "What was Jason *playing* at?"

"There's more." Bethany winced. "Are you okay for me to go on?"

"Christ. Yes." Warren sifted hair through his fingers. "You okay, Mum?"

Liz nodded.

"His browsing history would have had him arrested for having an unnatural predilection." Bethany paused, waiting for one of them to stop her carrying on.

They didn't.

"Don't tell me it's young girls," Warren said, stopping his back and forth across the carpet. He stared at Bethany. "Oh God, it is, isn't it?"

She nodded.

"My brother was a *nonce*?" He grabbed his hair in both hands, tugging it and growling.

The sound tore at Bethany's heart. "I'm so sorry. It'll come out in court once the suspect has been apprehended, probably the news, too, if there's a leak before the trial, so it's best you hear it from us first."

Liz rocked, hugging herself and staring at nothing. Warren went to her again and stroked her head.

"We really do have to go," Bethany said. "I'm sorry we can't stay."

"No, no, you need to get on with your job." Warren sat on the bed next to Liz. "We'll be fine."

She doubted Liz would, but that couldn't be her concern. She had to find Timothy Bishway and have a look at his nails.

They left the hotel and got in the car.

"Where the fuck can Timothy be?" she said, starting the engine then driving off.

"Try his house again, and I'll ring the RSPCA centre now to see if he's gone to work regardless of having a day off. Then we'll go to see his mother again."

She headed out of town, listening to Mike on the phone.

He shook his head once the call had ended. "No luck."

"We'll find him at some point, but I want to get him quick in case he goes after someone else."

She kept quiet then, trying to put herself in Timothy's shoes. Where would she go after killing people? Who else would be on her list? Pulling up to the kerb, she got out, and they walked to the front door. Bethany knocked, and the door swung open. Who she assumed was Cassandra Volten stood there, a holdall in hand.

"Oh, hi," she said. "Ben told me to stay elsewhere for a few days, so I'm just off. Had to pack a bag. I'm going to his girlfriend's."

"Is Timothy in?" Bethany asked.

"Not now, but he has been. The cheeky sod used my towel. It's wet in his room."

"Can I have a quick look in the bathroom?"

"Yep, help yourself." Cassandra dropped her bag on the floor.

Bethany and Mike went up the stairs, into the bathroom. She peered at the bath. It still had water droplets on the bottom.

"Did you have a shower?" she called down to Cassandra.

"No, Timothy must have. Like I said, he nicked my towel."

"Do you mind if we check his room?"

"Nope. Shall I shut the front door?"

"Probably best to. Lock it, will you? And stay put."

"Should we get a warrant?" Mike said.

"Fuck it, she gave us permission."

They entered Timothy's room, a pink towel, damp, on the bed. Bethany and Mike took gloves out of their pockets and put them on, then got to work opening drawers and the clothes cupboard. While Bethany checked all the jacket and jeans pockets, Mike got down on his knees and peered under the bed. She finished her task and reached down into the far corner at the bottom. A small jam jar was wedged between two shoes.

"I think I have something." She picked it up and stood. Stared at it. "Fucking hell."

She glanced at Mike, who looked up at her on his hands and knees.

"Teeth?" he said.

"Jason's?" She placed the jar down, her nerves pinging.

"I feel a bit sick." Mike carried on poking about under the bed. He drew a plastic bag out, one used to line bins. Ripping it, he tugged it open.

"Um, there are wet clothes in here, along with a disposable razor and some empty loo rolls," he said.

"Wet?"

"Hmm." He pulled out a white T-shirt. Pink stains marred the front. "Oh shit. Hang on, I think I've found the boots — or one pair anyway." He slid them out. Blood stained the laces.

Bethany got her phone out and rang Isabelle. "We need SOCO here at Timothy Bishway's new address." She recited it. "Clothes in a bag, what looks like faint blood on them. Teeth in a jar, and boots. We need the house going over in case he's hidden something else."

"Righty oh."

She slid her phone in her pocket. "Leave that there, Mike." She pointed at the bag. "We'd best get out as we haven't got booties on."

Downstairs, she advised Cassandra to definitely stay away, saying the house was now a scene of interest. "If Timothy gets hold of you, don't answer your phone."

"He hasn't got my number anyway."

"Good."

While the shocked woman walked out and to her car, Mike following to make sure she got off all right, Bethany's phone rang. Fran's name was on the screen.

"Hi," Fran said. "We've got the landline information back from Jason's and Opal's."

"And?"

"They were both called by the same number several times."

"Whose is it?"

"The BT account is in the name of Ben Chadwell at Timothy Bishway's new address."

"Excellent. Did you put in for the calls made to Nancy Forrester?"

"Yes, another day on that before they'll get the info to us. Kribbs sent off for the paperwork."

"Great. We're at Timothy's now, waiting for SOCO." She explained what had been found. "So now we're going to his mother's house yet again to see if he's there. Speak soon."

Mike came back in, and they waited in the hallway until four SOCOs and some uniforms arrived. Leaving them to it, she got in the car, Mike beside her, and drove to the Bishway's. On the doorstep, Bethany knocked, but no one answered, so she bent over and opened the letterbox.

"Oh fuck," she said, peering harder.

"What's the matter?" Mike asked, crouching.

"Looks like William's been battered. He's on the floor in the kitchen, blood everywhere." She moved across so Mike could see for himself.

"Shit," he said.

She rang Isabelle and asked for more SOCO and uniforms. Mike checked the door handle. It moved down, and he rushed inside then came back out.

"He's dead."

"Shit."

Bethany walked to the end of the path to stare up at the room she knew to be Harriet's. Had she killed her husband and was now in bed as though nothing had happened?

SOCO arrived and went inside.

Movement to her left caught her attention, and she turned her head to stare at the living room window next door. The net curtain swung where someone had maybe pulled it across to peer out then had let it go.

"Bloody nosy neighbours," she grumbled.

Then the door opened, and a woman ran out, blood dripping down her face from an unseen wound. "Help me," she screamed, racing down her path. "He's fucking mad!"

"Who's mad?" Bethany asked, rushing to her.

"Timothy. He tried to kill me."

CHAPTER TWENTY-THREE

Mike shouted into the Bishway's house for a SOCO to come and help. Bethany dashed up the path to the house the woman had come out of and dashed inside, her heart hammering way too fast. Mike brought up the rear, and together they entered the living room on the left. With no one in there, they moved to the back where a door led to a kitchen. A quick glance around showed no sign in him there either, but the door to the garden was ajar.

She moved to it and looked outside.

Timothy had ripped one end of the length of washing line down, looped it around his neck, and currently hung from the fence post, knees bent, feet on the patio. Bethany legged it out there, conscious this might be a trick and he'd jab her with a weapon once she got close.

"Fuck!" Mike said behind her and pushed ahead, lifting Timothy and draping him over his shoulder.

A SOCO barged outside.

"Call an ambulance," Bethany shouted, going over to pull the loop from around Timothy's neck. It seemed to take ages, her hands shaking, fingers like sausages, but it eventually came away.

Mike placed him on the patio and listened for Timothy's breathing. "He's alive." He stood, taking a step back.

"Thank Christ for that," she said, wiping her forehead.

They moved to stand by the door, leaving Timothy there. She didn't want to be anywhere near him if she could help it. He opened his eyes and glared at her, a creepy smile forming. A shudder rippled through her. Why hadn't she noticed his mad eyes before? He sat, then pushed to his feet.

Had he been faking the hanging? If so, why had he stayed where he was over Mike's shoulder instead of dropping down to make an escape? What agenda did he have?

"Stay there," she said. Shit, why hadn't they cuffed him already? "Turn around."

He stared for a while then did what she'd said.

"Hands behind your back," she ordered.

He obeyed.

Why is he complying? Had all the fight gone out of him? Did he realise this was the end of the line now and had accepted defeat? It all seemed too easy.

Mike stepped forward, cuffs in hand, and reached out, ready to secure them on Timothy's wrists, but Timothy whipped round and struck, the side of his fist catching Mike's temple. Mike grunted and staggered away, clutching his head. Bethany darted forward, banging into Timothy, who went down, whacking his hip on the slabs. The forward momentum had her surging onwards, and she used all her strength to pull back to stop herself from joining him on the ground. Adrenaline spiking, she stared at him as he shot up and lunged towards her, his face screwed up, anger radiating off him.

"You fucking bitch," he said, hands out at neck level.

His nails were wonky and ridged.

Mike darted behind him, appearing dazed from the punch, and pushed Timothy to the side. They both fell down, struggling against each other, rolling over and over until they hit the grass. Bethany ran to them and helped Mike pin him down, getting a smack to the nose for her trouble. Liquid heat oozed, and she cuffed her nostrils to wipe the blood away. Mike turned Timothy onto his front and wrenched his arms behind his back, Timothy bucking all the while. Wrists secure, he growled, an animalistic sound that sent chills through Bethany.

She got up, wiping her nose again, which had stopped dripping, backing away a step while Mike pushed to his feet. Together, they gripped an arm each and hauled Timothy upright. The SOCO came back.

"Can you do me a favour and ring for a meat wagon?" she said to him.

The SOCO nodded. "Our man?" He got his phone out.

"Yes. This prick here thought it would be amusing to play a joke on us," Bethany said. "He didn't hang himself at all."

"Who are you calling a fucking prick?" Timothy said, then spat in her face.

The SOCO went inside, phone pressed to his ear.

She cleaned the spittle off with her sleeve, acting as though what Timothy had done didn't bother her in the slightest, but inside her stomach churned. "You." She looked him up and down, eyeing the state of his clothing. It must have come from the woman who lived here. "Like wearing blood, do you?"

He stared her straight in the eyes. "Do you? There's a fair bit on your face."

Anger burned a path inside her, surging up in the form of words. "You, mate, are a fucking bastard."

"Like father, like son," he said, "although I did what I did for a reason." Timothy's sneer was cold, his eyes calculating.

"What bloody reason did you have to kill people?" she asked, shaking her head.

"I did it for Chelsea."

"And for yourself," she snapped. "Don't try to lay it all at your poor sister's door. Come on, I've had enough."

They had to drag him through the house — he refused to walk, going limp — and by the time they emerged onto the street, Bethany's arms ached from holding him up. She pressed him down into a sitting position onto the grass verge between the path and the road while they waited for the van to turn up.

"You found them then?" Timothy said, nodding at the open front door of his parents' house.

"Them?" Bethany cursed herself for letting him know she hadn't been aware there was a *them*, just a *he*, William Bishway.

"She's in bed." Timothy laughed then, his head dropping back, tears falling into the hair at his temples. The man was sodding delirious.

"Your mother, I take it," she said. "How did you kill her then?"

"A pillow." He curled up at that, teetering over onto his side and roaring his head off in the foetal position.

Bethany glanced at Mike and mouthed, "What the fuck?"

He shrugged.

Timothy was clearly off his rocker, and if the doctor didn't clear him to be interviewed, she wouldn't get her pound of flesh by making him suffer through questioning. Mind you, she didn't much fancy sitting across a table from him, listening to his excuses, seeing his crazy eyes glinting with malice.

They stood there while he continued laughing, seemingly unable to stop himself. She'd seen this before, when someone broken dipped into hilarity hysteria instead of crying. While she'd gathered he hadn't had the best of upbringings, she couldn't understand his need to kill. Was it his way of getting justice? The only way he could make himself feel better after the loss of his sister? Had her death sent him mad?

The wagon pulled up, and two officers jumped out, taking over possession of Timothy. They hefted him to the van and put him inside, the laughter still ongoing, drifting out eerily. Bethany shivered and rubbed her arms. Despite the heat of the day, she was damn cold. The van doors slammed shut, and she turned away from the vehicle to spot the woman who'd run out of the house. She sat on her garden wall, a uniform beside her.

"Are you all right, love?" Bethany asked, stepping over to her. "What's your name?"

"Annabelle Pellbody."

"The ambulance will be here soon. We need you to get checked over. You've got a nasty gash on your head there."

Annabelle raised her hand to touch it and winced. "He hit me with a full wine bottle."

Bethany grimaced. "What on earth went on? How did he even get into your house?"

Annabelle hung her head, staring at the pavement. "I opened the door, and he said he needed some paracetamol for his dad. William. I went inside to get it, leaving the door open, and the next thing I know, he's there, right behind me in the kitchen, holding a bag." She shuddered. "He started saying weird stuff, like how I shouldn't have been seeing his dad all these years. William was round mine all day, and I gathered Timothy knew."

Bethany raised her eyebrows at Mike. "Go on."

"I didn't know what to say to Timothy. I mean, he knew I was seeing Will. I sort of let it slip once when Chelsea broke her arm. I shouldn't have, I realised that straight after, but I was a bit of a gobby cow back then. But I love Will, and he loves me. We're going to be together soon, once he's broken the news to Harriet."

"What do you know about their marriage?" Bethany asked.

"Only that she's always in bed, but I swear to God I hear music and singing coming from there most days. Will says it can't be her because she's basically only able to get herself to the loo and hasn't got much energy to speak, let alone sing, but I heard her singing today, and so did he. But he reckons she hurts herself, says it's got to be her because he hasn't hit her. Okay, he's been a bastard to the kids over the years, but that's from the stress of his shitty marriage. Not that I condone it. The hitting."

"I see. Did he not think to get her psychiatric help?"

"I don't know."

"What about Timothy's and Chelsea's upbringing? What was that like?"

"He admitted he was horrible to them. I've heard him shouting at them many a time. Will went out to work and expected a meal every night, regardless of whether his kids cooked it. Timothy did a lot of the cleaning. I used to see him hanging the washing out, and Chelsea used to hand him the pegs. Always pink, they were."

A piece of the puzzle slotted into place, and a shiver rippled up Bethany's spine.

"Why would you want to be with a man like that?" Bethany asked.

Annabelle raised her head and made eye contact. "I can't help it. I love him."

For fuck's sake . . .

The ambulance drew up to the kerb, and Bethany wondered whether she ought to tell Annabelle now or wait until the crew had seen to her. The latter won.

"I'll leave you to get on with your check-up, then I'll be back to have another word."

She grabbed a wet wipe out of the ambulance for the blood on her face and washed it, then walked away with Mike, up the Bishway's path, where they put on protective clothing and stepped inside. She walked along the hall to where Isabelle stood staring down at William's body in the kitchen.

"I came here from Georgia's site," she said. "Left my assistant to oversee things there."

Bethany smiled. "Weapon use?"

"Over there." Isabelle pointed behind her to a baseball bat lying close to the bottom of a floor cupboard. "He's had quite a bashing."

Bethany looked down. William was unrecognisable, blood all over his wrecked face. His nose had been hit so hard it no longer stuck out and was flat, level with his cheeks.

“Oh, before I forget,” Isabelle said, “I had a call from one of the SOCOs at Timothy’s place. They found T-shirt print templates hidden behind his headboard, skulls already drawn on the white ones, eyes on the red.”

Bethany sighed. “Good. Hopefully the blood on those wet clothes belongs to Georgia.”

“Want to come and see the body upstairs?” Isabelle cocked her head.

Bethany nodded, and they all trooped to the bedroom where Harriet had played her sick game of pretending to be ill — although she had been, with a mental illness that had gone untreated. Bethany just didn’t get why William hadn’t done anything about it. Why wouldn’t he want to help a woman who harmed herself the way she had?

They all stood beside the bed.

“Looks to me like she was suffocated with a pillow,” Isabelle said, “but we’ll know more when Presley gets here. The signs are there, though.”

Bethany took a closer look. Red dots marred Harriet’s face, and her eyes bulged, so many red veins streaking the white. Her blue lips gave Bethany the creeps, and she stepped back, turning away to gaze around the room instead.

“A hell of a job you’ve got ahead you, patching all this together into a coherent wedge of paperwork for the CPS,” Isabelle said. “Although I can’t see them saying no to this going to trial.”

“No, there’s too much evidence.” Bethany let out a long, shuddery breath. “I’m so glad it’s over. And I don’t even think we’re going to get to interview him and ask him why he did this. Okay, he’s told us it was for Chelsea, but really? Running around killing people for your sister, who isn’t even here to know what you’ve done?”

“Why can’t you interview him?” Isabelle asked.

“I have a strong feeling he’s mentally unstable.”

“Oh. That’s harsh for you and for him.”

“Hmm.”

They left the room and went downstairs, and Bethany steeled herself to break the news about William's death to Annabelle Pellbody. Out in the street, she stared into the back of the ambulance. A paramedic patted Annabelle on the shoulder, then helped her out into the street.

"Is she all right?" Bethany asked.

The paramedic nodded. "Chicken egg on the head, and the blood came from a couple of deep gouges on her forehead where nails had been raked down her face."

Bethany hadn't noticed that beneath Annabelle's fringe, just the streaks of blood that must have dripped down. "Thanks."

She guided Annabelle inside her house and sat her on the sofa. Then she told her the news, and Annabelle's scream? Well, Bethany reckoned it would stay with her for many years to come.

* * *

By the time they made it back to the station, Timothy had had a medical assessment. He'd been taken to a secure facility, where, in time, he'd be questioned gently by trained psychiatrists. As Bethany had suspected, the man's mind was broken, and there was no satisfaction to be had in getting answers out of him themselves.

She brought Fran and Leona up to date, and tomorrow, they'd get to work compiling all the evidence, the statements, and filling out the paperwork. It was hard to believe one man had wreaked such havoc, but if he'd done it because of his rotten childhood and the fact that a bloke had got his underage sister pregnant, at least he'd had a genuine reason. Some people didn't and just killed for the hell of it.

Bethany went to her office and slumped in her chair, thinking about when Timothy had spat on her. Still, at least it wasn't shit. She'd had that lobbed at her on two occasions from men in the holding cells. You had to look on the bright side, didn't you?

Her mobile rang, and she smiled. Vinny's name on the screen. She glanced at the time, gobsmacked it was eight o'clock already. He must be calling her from the fire station.

"Hello, you lovely beast," she said, grinning her head off, imagining his reaction, wanting to hear him laugh so it meant he wasn't so down now.

"Um, Beth, it's Cuppa." He was Vinny's workmate, called that because he drank endless cups of tea all day.

"Oh. Hello. Err, why are you using Vinny's phone?"

"Are you sitting down, love?" he asked.

Oh God. No. This couldn't be the call she'd always dreaded. "Has he been hurt?" she asked, her heart thundering so hard it was painful.

"There was a fire. Out of control," Cuppa said. "He went in when it was deemed unsafe by the chief, and . . ."

"No. *No.* Don't you be fucking telling me that." She shot to her feet, pacing, her mind going a mile a minute. "What hospital is he in? The small one or the big one?" It had to be the big one, didn't it, for burns?

"The big one. Beth, he's—"

She didn't give him a chance to finish. Cutting the call, she ran out of her office and into the incident room. Only Mike remained, sitting at his desk reading over a statement. He turned and looked at her and must have registered something was wrong, because he was over to her in seconds, hands pressed to her shoulders.

"What the fuck's happened?" he asked, dipping his head to look into her eyes.

"It's Vinny," she managed, her throat going tight. "A fire. He . . . he went in when he shouldn't have."

"Christ Almighty. Who do I ring for information?"

She handed him her phone. "Cuppa rang me from Vinny's mobile."

He took it from her and walked out, leaving her to stagger to a chair and fall onto it. Her beautiful Vinny couldn't be all burnt, could he? He didn't deserve to get hurt like that, not when he cared so much about the people he battled to save. Not when he carried their deaths around with him for weeks afterwards, blaming himself the way he did.

Mike's voice filtered in from the corridor, mumbles, his tone so low she couldn't make out what he said. He'd go with her to see Vinny in the hospital, she wouldn't have to do it alone. And once Vinny was better, she'd ask him to think about whether he should continue in his line of work. It wasn't safe, he got depressed, so surely it was better all round if he did something else. Today he'd been burnt, but what about the future? What if he died and—

No. She wouldn't think about that.

But she had to, because Mike came back in, and his face said it all. "Oh, love . . ."

Bethany's scream answered him.

EPILOGUE

The funeral had been a celebration of Vinny's life, but Bethany didn't want to celebrate it. No, she wanted to rail, to scream, to tear her fucking hair out. This wasn't what was supposed to have happened. They were meant to grow old with each other, to have lived a long and full life, side by side, not her walking their path alone. In her mind's eye, it stretched ahead of her, winding and lonely, every twist and turn taking her farther away from their time together, into a future without him.

She remembered her thoughts when Jason Holt had been killed, how Georgia must have been feeling. How Bethany knew she'd have to throw herself into work if she ever lost Vinny.

Well, now she had.

Was this even happening? It was all so surreal, as though she watched everything from outside herself, the murmured words from mourners coming at her as if from far away. Their mouths moved, and she struggled to lip read, but one word had been said more than any other.

Sorry.

There was no one sorrier than her.

She glanced around the graveyard, with the flowers either side of the rectangle cut out of the ground where Vinny's coffin had been lowered. The sun shone, the obscene, rude bastard, when it should be raining, Heaven sending down God's tears to mesh with hers.

At last, she stood there alone.

Everyone but Mike had gone to the wake, which had been set up in the local hall on Bethany's housing estate, seeing as there were so many people in attendance, even some Vinny had saved in fires.

He'd gone running into that building to rescue a baby. A family home, where a chip pan had caught fire, and the mother, father, and older son had got out, both parents thinking the other had gone upstairs to collect the baby girl. By the time they'd realised their mistake, the fire had consumed the lower floor, and the father had made to go inside, but neighbours had held him back. And he'd screamed.

Not half as much as I did when I got the news.

Vinny and the crew had arrived, and by then the flames had engulfed the whole house. The roof was caving in, rafters breaking, jutting out at odd angles from beneath the tiles that seemed to have just melted away. And Vinny had gone in, regardless of what he'd been told, his kind, beautiful heart insisting that he could save that baby and bring her out to her parents.

When the fire had been put out, his body had been found beside the cot, his arm through the bars, his hand holding the child's.

She sighed, her chest juddering, a part of her wishing he hadn't been so goddamned compassionate and had for once thought of himself, of her, before he'd made that split-second decision that had robbed him of his life and given her a prison sentence of sorts, because living without him would be just like incarceration.

"We didn't get a chance to do everything, did we, Vin," she said to the coffin, the silver plaque on it glinting in the sunlight. "We promised we wouldn't put ourselves in too much danger, and now look at us. You're down there, I'm up here, and God, I wish I was in there with you."

The teak box remained silent, of course it did, and she gazed at it, unable to believe her husband was in it. It seemed too small, too narrow.

A slight breeze ruffled the flowers, wafting their scent to her, and her eyes burned, tears falling once again. Her body felt hollow, her heart empty of love — Vinny had taken it all with him. How the hell she was going to get through this mad thing called life without him, she didn't know.

Work, she supposed.

She turned away and walked towards the path, unable to say goodbye, even at this stage of his passing. If she said farewell, it meant it was real, and she was damned if she could face that yet. One day, when the grief wasn't so raw, maybe then she could let him go. For now, she'd push herself through the days as best she could, waiting for a time when it didn't hurt so much.

She had the urge to do something, to break out of this lethargy that had consumed her in the fortnight since his death. If she didn't, she'd take to her bed like Harriet Bishway and hide beneath her quilt, slowly going mad.

Mike got out of his car and came towards her, his face wreathed in concern. He didn't say a word, just held his arm out, and she let him rest it over her shoulder. She seemed to float to his vehicle, in some kind of fog, him all but glued to her side, and she wondered what he was thinking, whether he didn't know what to say to her.

She looked up at his face and managed a small smile.

"I'm here," he said. "I'm here."

She remembered saying that to him recently.

And he *was* here, always had been.

He drove them away from the cemetery, towards her estate, and she took a deep breath. Right now was the real start of widowhood, a whole new world she hadn't anticipated living in until she was in her eighties. But, here she was, thrust into it, and she'd better just make the best of it, really, until she could see Vinny again. She was on leave for another couple of weeks, a whole month in total, and it was going to drive her mental.

Too much time to dwell. To think.

She wouldn't be able to hack it.

She'd ask Kribbs if she could come back tomorrow. He'd understand.

Mike's phone rang, giving her a jolt, and he pulled over and answered it.

"Yep. *What*? You're kidding me." He turned to face Bethany, eyes wide.

"What's the matter?" she said, sensing something was wrong.

"A body," he said. "At the bottom of someone's garden."

"What?" She sat up straighter, latching on to this information like a lifeline, anything to keep her mind off her shitty predicament. "Where?"

Mike asked whoever was on the end of the line, then said to her, "Three streets away."

"Then let's go," she said, slapping the dashboard. "Now!"

Mike's mouth hung open. "But the wake . . ."

"Fuck the wake. Vinny wouldn't want me moping about there. He'd want me to get on with things, to go and sort this out. Look how he was when he lost people at work. Do you think he'd rather I didn't go and throw myself into this?" She inhaled a deep breath. Let it out. Gathered her mettle. "Well, come on! What are you waiting for? Drive on, partner."

And she swore Vinny cheered somewhere, the sound of his voice telling her she'd made the right decision. To thrust herself into work. To cope. To manage without him.

I'm doing this for you, Vin. Only you.

THE END

THE JOFFE BOOKS STORY

We began in 2014 when Jasper agreed to publish his mum's much-rejected romance novel and it became a bestseller.

Since then we've grown into the largest independent publisher in the UK. We're extremely proud to publish some of the very best writers in the world, including Joy Ellis, Faith Martin, Caro Ramsay, Helen Forrester, Simon Brett and Robert Goddard. Everyone at Joffe Books loves reading and we never forget that it all begins with the magic of an author telling a story.

We are proud to publish talented first-time authors, as well as established writers whose books we love introducing to a new generation of readers.

We have been shortlisted for Independent Publisher of the Year at the British Book Awards three times, in 2020, 2021 and 2022, and for the Diversity and Inclusivity Award at the Independent Publishing Awards in 2022.

We built this company with your help, and we love to hear from you, so please email us about absolutely anything bookish at: feedback@joffebooks.com.

If you want to receive free books every Friday and hear about all our new releases, join our mailing list: www.joffebooks.com/contact

And when you tell your friends about us, just remember: it's pronounced Joffe as in coffee or toffee!

ALSO BY EMMY ELLIS

DI BETHANY SMITH
Book 1: THE COLD CALL KILLER

DETECTIVE CAROL WREN MYSTERIES
Book 1: SPITE YOUR FACE
Book 2: HOLD YOUR BREATH
Book 3: GUILT BURNS HOLES
Book 4: BEST SERVED COLD
Book 5: BLOOD RUNS DEEP

Printed in Great Britain
by Amazon

42171356R00111